I0671563

EMPIRE ALL IN

A Novel of the Trump Era

Tony Christini

BADAK MERAH SEMESTA

2017

EMPIRE ALL IN
A Novel of the Trump Era

Cover Art by: WPA poster by Julius Pistchal

Cover Design by: Rossie Indira

Layout by: Rossie Indira

First edition, 2017

Published by PT. Badak Merah Semesta

Jl. Madrasah Azziyadah 16, Jakarta

http://badak-merah.weebly.com

email: badak.merah.press@gmail.com

ISBN: 978-602-73543-7-1

Tony Christini

CONTENTS

Tony Christini

CHAPTER ONE

Tony Christini

Death by Texas

*T*exas? Our Texas? asked Presidential Aide Dineh.

Stupid! Idiot! Losers! The illegals are killing us! I will make America great again! cried President Donbo King Tyrump. He pounded a map on the wall with his fist. It's destiny!

The Invasion of Texas was on.

The day of his inauguration as President of the United States of America, President Tyrump ordered a map of the world hung on the wall by his desk in the Oval Office.

While killing time between rounds of golf, he showed the map to his Presidential aide, Dineh.

President Tyrump thumped Texas with his fist three times, then once more for emphasis.

This! Dineh! Look! It's destiny! Manifest! Whatever that means! I will make my America great again! There's border land there, Dineh, and I'm taking it! Only the Great Wall of Texas will keep the illegals out! I'll build a border wall mall casino resort and make the big bucks on both sides of the wall! A great big beautiful border wall mall! Never surrender! Remember

1

the Alamo! Damn outlaws! I'll line the Rio Grande with golf courses and Texas Hold 'Em poker tables and make it its own long country: Tyrumplandia! Brand Tyrump! We'll extend the Tyrump wall mall casino and resort all across Earth! It will be a great show! People like shows, Dineh! I know I do! Especially the ones where I star! I love the glitz and glitter, glory and glam! Good times, Dineh! We only have to stop the illegals at the border to make all my dreams come true!

Mr. President, what about the people who already own that border land, Sir? They won't give it up without a fight. Not for a great wall, or a grand mall, or anything.

Then a fight they will get, Dineh! That's why we are invading Texas! You start by seizing the land! You bring in guns and take whatever else you might! Take it all if need be! Whatever there is to take, you get! Whatever I need that I don't already have becomes mine! The border wall is merely the beginning!

Mr. President, there are native tribes along the border that will fight you, I'm sure of it. And some people have land rights going all the way back to Spain, the Spanish land grants, Sir.

So we bomb Spain too, what's the big deal? And the Natives?! What do they know about fighting for land? Are they any good at it? Why are they still around? Why are the Natives always standing in the way of progress, Dineh?! Have they no respect for the people of this land?! Tell me, Dineh, you're Native: look how well you adapted to the ways of the world. Why are these throwback Natives trying to stop my rightful rule, trying to destroy my name, blocking my oil and gas pipelines in the Dakotas! Threatening my border wall in the Southwest! Fighting fracking in my Empire State of New York?! Do they ever win?! If they don't ever win, why do they keep fighting, Dineh?! Tell me!

There's no fracking in New York state, Sir.

For now! Only for now, Dineh!

For years now, Mr. President.

That's why the Natives must be overthrown, Dineh! They're everywhere! Fighting civilization tooth and nail! They're like babies! Babbling on about their precious water! Water?! What is water worth to Wall Street?! Nothing, Dineh! Or next to it! Don't these Natives know they need to be civil? You tell them, Dineh! You should solve the problem, the Native problem! What exactly is their problem, anyway?! What's wrong with these people?!

Mr. President, some people see things differently than other people, Sir. Is there a Native problem, or is there a White Man problem? That's how some people see it. You want to take the Texas border. Some people don't want to give it up. More than 6 in 10 Texans oppose building the border wall, Sir. About the same as last year, Mr. President. So what is the White Man problem in Texas? Some people say that, Sir.

Whites are not the problem, Dineh, don't be stupid! Native Supremacy is the problem! And

Black Supremacy too! And Brown Supremacy! And what other colors are there?! Yellow Supremacy!

Yellow Supremacy, Mr. President?

The environmentalists, Dineh, who else?! They're always going on about the power of the sun. It gets old.

I see. Maybe it's a Dollar problem, Sir.

There's only one way to see things, Dineh! My way, or you can put it on the road, Son. Great leaders lead, and the people follow! All the people! Why can't everyone learn this simple truth of history?!

It's a mystery, Sir. A lot of Texans will fight this border wall, already are. They see the land as their land, and not your land, and they don't want a wall on it, through, or over. They don't want a wall between them and the river, or between them and their history, or between them and their families, or between them and the rest of the land, Sir.

They are uncivilized, Dineh! I tell you, outlaws! No one will side with these criminals! Terrible Texans! I will get my fabulous Press Secretary, Mr. Bullcrap Baloney Bullshat to explain reality yet again! No one can tell the story of the world better than Secretary Bullshat. I picked him for the job myself. Bullcrap and I see eye to eye. Bullcrap always says the right thing. He has to or he's history. I'll take care of that. Don't be history, Dineh! Make history! History loves winners. History hates Losers. And Losers are haters. It's sick. And boy do I hate Losers,

Dineh!

Mr. President, regarding the history of the border in Texas and beyond, Sir, what a lot of people say is that they did not cross the border, the border crossed them. They don't think they are on the wrong side of the border, not on either side. And they don't think a wall will work. There are ladders, Sir. Tunnels. Planes. Hammers. Agents who take bribes, or, you know, have a heart, Sir. And some people, Mr. President, see a border wall as a 12th century solution to a space age situation, Sir.

It's outer space, all right! Illegal aliens, Dineh! The border hasn't crossed anyone but me, especially me! Me, not them! I'm the one who has been crossed! The border makes me very cross! I'm going to wall it all off, if it's the last thing I do! The Great Wall of Texas! I will stop the illegals in their alien tracks. I will conquer all Texas to do it, if I must! And I must! I'm a winner, Dineh. It's all I know. For me there is no other way to live than to win. The wall is a winning idea, don't doubt me. These illegal alien outlaws must be stopped in their tracks!

Mexicans, Central Americans and others have fled economies wrecked by, well, they say by NAFTA, Sir, the North American Free Trade Agreement, and by US Imperialism, Mr. President. They say NAFTA was great for investors but not so good for workers on either side of the border. Not so good at all, Sir. They say the trade deals trade away workers' rights for investors' rights.

The illegals are conquistadors, Dineh! Nothing more. They are trying to conquer our homeland! Who cannot see that?! These alien outlaws would get rid of NAFTA and waste our money on themselves! It's a tragedy, a crime against humanity! Against our planet! Against our way of life! Against our children, Dineh! Why do you think the illegals are always trying to take care of our children in our homes? To brainwash them! That's the invasion right there, Dineh! The invasion of the mind snatchers! And it's a disaster for our dollars! The bankers will not stand for it! White people don't like it! The invasion stops now! We will seal off the border, we will take Texas to save it, and we will keep America American! White makes right makes might makes...whatever, a lot of good things, Dineh! Believe me. History is ours, not theirs.

I'm not white, Sir.

You're not in charge! You are under command and control here, Dineh! I get to make the history around these parts, around the globe! History is mine, by right!

That gets back to the border, Sir, and whose lands are whose. It gets to how everyone sees history, Mr. President, the reality on the ground.

Give it up, Dineh. You're no Press Secretary Bullcrap Baloney Bullshat! I tell you that. Reality is what I say it is! You are merely my personal bottle aide! Your job is to get me my special nasal inhalers when I must have them most! I don't need you to stand there and dissect policy willy-nilly! Any group of fools can do that! Have you seen my Cabinet?! I need you to monitor my daily nasal inhaler needs. That's all!

Yes, Sir, Mr. President. I apologize. I don't know what I was thinking.

Don't make me fire you, Dineh! And don't think! It's bad for the digestion. My digestion for sure. It's not what it used to be. Thank heavens for those little bottles of joy you serve up so well! My sweet tea! Tyrump's T!

Only as prescribed, Mr. President. Your special medicine. Free, universal health care, Sir, for everyone, why not? Other countries do it. It saves money. It would help so many. It would be a relief to business. The health of the people would dramatically improve, Sir. Costs would go way down. People could live much better, Mr. President.

People, Dineh?! This isn't a place for people! I'm a businessman, did you forget?! The business of business is business! People have no business interfering! Who do you think I am? Who do you think you are talking to, right now? I'm in the billionaire business, Dineh! I'm the one who fokkks! I own the USA! And the world! You've seen my cabinet. They're billionaires, Buddy, or soon to be! And Congress! The majority of Congress are millionaires, only, but put it in perspective, Dineh! You clearly don't know who you're talking to, so let me clue you in. Do you think I'm your friend? I'm your Master! I own you! Do you want me to fire you so soon, Dineh?! You only just got on this show! Business is what I do! Have you lost all respect for the Incorporated

Estates of Earth?!

President Tryump picked up his handheld device from the top of the presidential desk and tapped out a tweet:

My aid Dinnay is a dumbass. But he serves well.

There, Dineh, look at that.

President Tyrump showed the tweet to his aide, Dineh.

I have 4 billion followers, Dineh. Give or take. The whole world. And now they know who you are. You can thank me later.

I see, Sir. I'm very sorry, Sir.

Say my name.

Sir?

Dineh, say my name.

You are President Tyrump, Sir.

Say it!

Tyrump! President Tyrump! President of the United States of America!

You're goddamn right I am.

I apologize again, Mr. President. Sir, it's only that I know you love a good repartee-

President Tyrump tossed his handheld onto the presidential desk.

I do love parties, Dineh. You got me there. Love to party. Love people. Love the people who love parties. The people I know are always there, at the parties. My people. The party people. You're not a terrible person, Dineh. You only act like it sometimes.

I am imperfect, Sir.

It's the illegals who spoil the parties, Dineh!

They slip in to serve and cart the food and drinks but we can't have them joining the party! What fun would that be?! They would ruin it for everyone, those criminals! Only criminals cross borders uninvited, Dineh! We have to stop it cold! We'll take over all Texas to flush them out!

Don't you think it's a problem, Sir, that millions of undocumented immigrants have lived here in this country for years and decades, working, paying taxes, sales taxes, gas taxes, this tax, that tax, and raising families? You don't think they feel at home here, Sir? They're already home. How do you deport people from their home?

Dineh, why do you make it sound like you are describing white people?

As illegals, Sir?

Those are the brown people! Who can be so blind?! Sometimes you make the white people sound brown and the brown people sound white! There's no logic to your words, Dineh!

I'm not talking about color, Sir.

You don't have to say it to say it, Dineh! We all know what things mean. You don't have to say what you mean to you say what you mean. Try to keep up, Dineh. I've got a world to rule. It's difficult for some people to understand. But I need you to know better because I need you to keep those little bottles flowing at the right time, Dineh! You need to try harder to get right with me and with Press Secretary Bullcrap Baloney Bullshat. He always clarifies things wonderfully. Listen closely to what he says and how he says it.

You don't want to wind up as a historic object of ridicule, Dineh! Trust me on this one. You wouldn't like it! The important thing to remember is that in our security system, everyone is a suspect until proven innocent, and even then! These are outlaw Texans, Mexicans, Guatemalans, who knows where they might come from, even if you ask them?! Sinners all. These are not saints on the loose looking to be baptized in the waters of the Rio Grande! These are women-grabbing, border-raping, money-grubbing, blowhard criminals! And we know what color they are! They are violent thug racists! Abusers of women! Sneaky law breaking flag wavers! I look in the mirror, Dineh, and I expect to see them sneaking up behind me!

Flag wavers, Sir?

You're right, Dineh. Scratch that. Flag haters! They don't know whose flag to wave! They take money from my country and send it away never to return until I launch the military to get back what is mine! With a little help from Exxon! All over the world, by God! The illegals would trade away our world for their own! They are freeloaders, Dineh! They breathe our free air! Every day! For free! They would bankrupt the banks to get what they want!

A job, Sir? Isn't that what they want?

Money, Dineh! Money is the root of their evil! They take all the jobs, even the jobs that nobody wants! They take those too! Especially those! Every first and last one of us pays the price for that greed, Dineh! Texas has always been full of lawlessness, people grabbing things away from everybody else. I shouldn't have to tell you any of this, Dineh! Pay attention to Press Secretary Bullcrap Baloney Bullshat! He knows, or can guess, every outlaw detail of Texas! Texas is a prime suspect and always has been! Texas is ripe for conquest! If we invade Texas now and take the whole damned thing, our poll ratings will spike, weapons sales will boom, bankers will rake in the money, contractors will rush in behind the bombs, an entire new world of goods and services will explode! The stimulus to all will be incredible! Conquered Texas will provide jobs for people from all over the country where work is scarce! Dollars will flow like gas and oil! Bombs will roll! The bankers will thrive! They always do!

At what cost, Mr. President? How do you conquer the entire land of Texas without first destroying it?

Precision blasting, Dineh! Who said anything about destroying anything?! I have a military filled with finely skilled technicians. They will refashion Texas. Bring it up to date. Turn it over to me and my allies in economics. Don't bother me with the details, Dineh! My money comes from the branding: Tyrump! I leave the demolition and hammer work to others.

Sir, if you send in the military, if you conquer Texas, if it really is to be rebuilt, wouldn't the profiteers hire have-not Mexicans from across the border: wall or no wall?

Profiteers?! Dineh, speak American.

Contractors, Sir. The contractors will hire have-not Mexicans from across the border. Mexico's economy, somehow, is worse than ours.

Freedom comes with a price, Dineh! But what is price to a boss dealer like myself?! I will gladly see it paid! I'll cut a great deal, someone will pay it. There's a sucker, Dineh, born every minute. Every second! Bull sharks like me eat suckers by the billions. I'll get someone to pay the cost of freedom, Dineh! You can bank on that. I do. We're not profiteers. We're businessmen.

President Donbo King Tyrump paced in front of the map of Texas.

The illegals! They cause us so much suffering! We'll invade Mexico the same time we take Texas, Dineh! Don't worry, we'll scare Mexico into walling in their own people. By threats. Dollar threats. Gun threats. The works. We'll force Mexico to build a second wall on their side of the border!

Two walls, Sir? Instead of repairing roads and bridges, schools and hospitals? Would even two walls be enough for you, Sir? Why not a third?

Excellent point, Dineh! It's true, we could use a third wall! But where would we put it?! Across the Canadian border! Oh, Canada!

I'm sorry, Sir - I'm sorry, Canada - I didn't mean to suggest-

Don't apologize, Dineh. Always complain, never explain! We should have grabbed that great idea by the bull horns long ago.

A wall against Canada, Sir? To stop

immigrants from the north?

To stop the air, Dineh! To stop the very air they breathe! We need to kill the cold air the socialists bathe in up there! We'll halt it at the border! The bitter Canadian air and all the socialist ideas threatening my way of life, Dineh. We'll build a really tall wall to block out those damned Arctic blasts! And Canada will pay for it! God, how I detest the polar vortex and the socialists who breed in it. Nature can be a terrible thing, Dineh, criminal! I hate the cold air and the cold socialists both! I hate them all! That's why I'm in favor of Climate Change! Global warming is the best! If things really get cooking I might not need to jet off to my Florida golf course so often. Nothing wrong with my golf course in New Jersey when the weather is good. Honest to God, Dineh, I don't see why some naysayers are so worried about Climate Change. The only climate I want to change is Canada's godforsaken weather and their bitter cold socialist fronts that threaten to overrun us all down here. Cold weather is socialist weather, Dineh! People start to huddle together and think they are all cozy. Goddamn Norway! With a third wall, a really tall wall, we can stop that crap at the border! Goddamn Sweden! People will vote for a Canadian wall, you watch. It might seem crazy but that's the vote we want, that and the rich vote. That's the vote that's out there for us, the only vote we want there to be out there, that's the vote we want! The rich and crazy vote. We have to get that vote, Dineh! Otherwise, we lose it to some wacko dollar wannabe like Hilty Crimeton! And what does she know about making money?! I can sell snow to Eskimos, Dineh, just give me some glitter, a snow machine, and godawful loud music! People love fake snow, Dineh. Cha-ching! Have you seen my casinos and resorts?! I'm the fake snow King of my World!

Mr. President, do you really think a third wall-

Who's thinking, Dineh?! We don't want too much of that going around. It can be contagious! Press Secretary Bullcrap Baloney Bullshat can spin all these great ideas to perfection! A wall against Canada doesn't have to work, Dineh, no wall really amounts to much in the end, ask the Chinese! Think about it! No, wait! Hold that thought! You don't need to trouble the old noggin, Dineh. Sometimes I do. Don't tell anyone. As long as a wall gets votes and dollars, dollars and votes, you make money and you win! I'm a winner, that's all there is, Dineh. No Loser ever won a damn thing.

I suppose not, Sir.

Not once. Losers don't win.

Well put, Sir. About Canada, I don't know, Mr. President, how socialist it actually is.

There's a sickness up there, Dineh. And we don't want that sickness spreading to our great system.

If you mean Canada's universal health care system, Sir, it does cover everyone all the time, and at much lower cost compared to ours, and the outcomes are pretty darn-

It would be lethal, Dineh. Fatal.

To whom, Sir?

To my way of life! To our country's well being!

How, Sir? Wouldn't it help all the people?

Too many people would be getting stuff that should be going to me, Dineh! The cruelty of your stupidity, Dineh, boggles the mind. The insanity of your ignorance, Dineh, is spectacular. Universal health care, medicine free for all would literally destroy this nation's very flag, Dineh. It would rip our identity to shreds. Mine especially! The flag, Dineh! We must save our flag and all that it stands for! Private corporate controlled insurance is next to Godliness! There can be no such thing as free medical treatment. Not under our beautiful, wonderful flag! Free health care for all would kill me and everyone around me! At least, it would kill my right to rule as I see fit! Defend the flag! No universal health care! God, what a beautiful flag we have, don't you think, Dineh? It makes my heart swell just to look at it! Those stripes and everything!

Have you seen the Navajo Nation flag, Mr. President? With the four colorful sacred mountains and the brilliant rainbow and the beautiful sand painting effect?

Come again, Dineh?! Whose nation?! Dineh, speak American!

Yes, Sir. I try to, Sir. You feel that you have a lot to lose, don't you, Mr. President?

My country, right and wrong, Dineh! My world! And I'm not a loser! Clearly! You don't understand, Dineh, because you don't have the worries that we billionaires do. A billionaire can never have too much. He has to worry about all the other billionaires taking his money! So he can't spare money for anyone else. I can't! Can't be done! There's not enough money in my country to go around to every damned debtor who would like to, you know, see a doctor, or something.

Or go to college, Sir, earn a living wage, afford a house, a car, raise a family, eat, heat, get off the street... Isn't that correct, Mr. President? Is that asking too much? If it is, then you're right, Sir, I don't understand. Other countries do it.

Socialist countries, Dineh. France, England, Germany, Canada. Show some patriotic pride, Dineh! My country right and wrong!

Sir, I think you mean-

I know exactly what I mean! How dare you think in front of me! Dineh, I will get a thrill when I fire you. As I will, one of these days. The sooner the better. But I'm about ready for a bottle, I think. That damned doctor should give me the code to my own bottles. I'll fire him too!

At your leisure, Mr. President.

President Tyrump picked up his phone and sent another tweet: Dinnay is still a dumbass. So dumb.

And then another: The President of China is a weenie!

Why did you do that, Mr. President?

I felt like it, Dineh. And I'm sure it's true. Anyway, this is how I negotiate. You knock a guy down first, then you take what he owes you. Who is the President of China, Dineh? Spell that.

Dineh spelled the Chinese President's name for President Tyrump who tried to follow but finally gave up and tweeted instead: The President of China - big country - little man.

Sir, the current Chinese President is the tallest man since Mao, Sir.

Mao who?! How much is he worth?! I don't care how tall the President of China is, Dineh. He's not going to be climbing any border wall!

True enough, Sir. I imagine he will fly over.

We'll track every inch of his flight path, Dineh.

I'm sure that will relieve everyone, Sir. Mr. President, regarding Mexico, I don't imagine that Mexico will wall itself in, no matter what story Press Secretary Bullshat comes up with.

Give it time, Dineh! That's what the threats are for! Mexico will do whatever we threaten it to do. That's all they know. They're used to it. They probably even like it. I don't hear too many complaints, do you? Who would listen anyhow?

You're aware, of course, Mr. President, that neither dollar threats nor gun threats are legal under international law.

Send me a memo the day it ever stops us, Dineh! Please. Is that some kind of sick joke? Show history some respect! I have to. As President, I get to decide who we invade and when. And then Press Secretary Bullcrap Baloney Bullshat makes up the stories to sell to whoever wants to be sold. You don't get to make up the stories, Dineh, you and your kind. That's not your problem, that's not your place, so don't worry about it. You're here to work for us. God forbid peaceniks rule the world. PeaceNukes rule! Is there something wrong with you today, Dineh?! Not enough sleep for the old noggin? You're acting like the National Political Police! I'm talking about invading Texas here! If I want the FBI up in my business, I'll order you to send them a memo too! After Texas, we take Mexico! International law is for Losers, Dineh! I don't care who the bigot judge is. By invasion or by threat of invasion, by munitions or by money, by fear and by force, by the People, of the People, for the People...what am I saying?! You know it. I know it. The whole damned world knows it. Every idiot LOSER knows it. The Invasion of Texas, that's reality. International law is for Losers, Dineh. It's make-believe.

You're serious then, Mr. President?

Plague serious, Dineh.

What about the animals trapped by the wall, Sir?

Rapists! Murderers! We'll catch them all!

Excuse me, Mr. President, I mean the wildlife. The creatures that need room to roam. Dineh tapped on his handheld and showed it to President Tyrump, who yanked the device from Dineh's hand. President Tyrump frowned at the screen.

What's this?! Ocelots and Jaguars and Jaguarundi?! Bobcats and Mountain Lions?! What are these things to me?!

Sir, these are threatened wildcats that live along the border. Your dear wife Myownia, she likes animals, doesn't she?

Myownia and cats? Women love cats! Myownia has a few nice tiger striped dresses and garments, fetching clothing, Dineh, I assure you. Myownia loves cats! But she loves walls too. Who doesn't love a great big wall to lean against? And mine is going to be a really Great Wall, clearcut wide on each side with a Border Patrol road the whole way from sea to shining sea, a big bad gun-lined highway that chain-links, brick mortars, cement binds, razor wires, laser lashes the Gulf of Mexico to the Pacific Ocean, the Great Wall of Texas! Electrified, strobelighted, whatever it takes, loudspeakers - hell, it could be a casino mall wall easy - with machine guns, cannons, and who knows what else you need to stop these people coming up from the south! We'll spare no detail! I'll keep the price down by making great deals, Dineh, great deals. In the end, Mexico will pay for it all! The wall mall will pay for itself! We'll put long rows of slot machines on either side! You can't cross but you can still get right with capitalism right there on the border! Who cares if we cut off the Rio Grande from our own country, dirty old river, we'll have the casino mall wall instead! Everyone will love it! Whatever we need on the Great Big Beautiful Fortified Electronified Militarized Wall of Texas, we'll get! We'll find some great American companies with super sales on parts and guns and things!

Not "Made in China," Sir? Because of the trade deals? It be would ironic, don't you think, if the Great Wall of Texas were to be built out of materials "Made in China" - like what you sell in your product lines, Sir: Tyrump! suits, Tyrump! ties, Tyrump! glasses, shirts, wallets-

That's all in the past, Dineh! I'm telling you! I mean, we need to look ahead, to the future, where who knows what might be?! Believe only this, Dineh: the future is ours! Mine!

So it would appear, Sir.

Don't doubt me!

Yes, Mr. President, about these wildcats that Myownia likes, Sir, their natural range and habitat is being cut in two by the border wall. And the cats' access to water, the rivers and springs, their food and drink and shelter, all gone, blocked off. A wall could wipe them out, Mr. President. So many animals are alive because of the rivers and streams through four states and two countries, Sir, across the continent. You're walling off two continents, the land and water, plants and animals, and of course people, Sir. You're caging in the people, Mr. President. On both sides. It's quite a blow to nature, Sir. And there are a lot of beautiful parks and walking trails along the river, Sir, which would all get chopped up, cut off. No more walking to and along the beautiful semi-tropical river, Sir.

To Hell with nature, Dineh! Too bad! Look around: nature is already trashed! Land, water, it's all disgusting until I get my brand on it: Tyrump! And what does it matter anyhow?!

Anything you break you can fix! No more to or from Mexico! Good riddance little kitty cats! The animals will have to choose sides, now, won't they?! What is it with you Natives and water, anyway, Dineh?!

Sir, if you will only look-

There's nothing more I want to see, Dineh! There's nothing else I need to see. None of these things on your twitter machine here!: the Barred Tiger Salamander! Stripes, great, but my dear Myownia doesn't like reptiles. Too slimy. And what's this?!: the Texas Horned Lizard! Very scaly. Now look at this one!: the Texas Earless Lizard. Earless! It doesn't even have ears, Dineh! It can't hear what we have to say! And see this slithering thing!: the Plains Blind Snake! It's blind! Snakes are Losers, Dineh, trust me, especially blind snakes! Who knew the border had all these deformed animals on it?! Who cares?! They must be from Mexico! Horned Lizards! Earless Lizards! Blind Snakes! And what's a Chachalaca?! It looks like a runt turkey. We've got plenty of American turkeys, Dineh, great big fat ones! Every Thanksgiving I order two or three, I don't even know how many, a lot, turkeys for my whole clan! We don't need Mexican turkeys in our country, Dineh. Oh great, and see here!: the Nine-banded Armadillo! It's a rat in a shell! And the Collared Peccary?! Fancy name for a pig on the loose! Put it behind bars where it belongs and can be happy and grow fat! Lots of pork in America, Dineh. There's pork everywhere. When we need pork, we get pork, we get all the pork we can handle! And the Rio Grande Chirping Frog? Who gives a chirp?! Oh, Christ! Look at that!: the Southern Yellow Bat, nothing but a flying vampire! Myownia is deathly afraid of vampires, her being born near Transylvania and all. This is terrifying, Dineh! All these deranged creepy crawlies on the border! Wildcats! Coyotes! Wolves! Oh, why?! Come to think of it, chopping up the border and cutting off the river to stop these dangerous deformed vagrants makes me realize that my idea of building a giant border wall is an even better idea than ever before! So thank you for that, Dineh! Myownia doesn't like vagrants either! Not since I've known her. She's a city girl. No cities on the border, Dineh, not real ones. Except San Diego, great golf courses, and San Diego is already walled off. You want animals, Dineh, go to a zoo. San Diego has a great zoo, I hear, all the animals can go there, if they have to go somewhere! Why not?! Zoos are where animals belong, so that people can see them! In safety, Dineh! In safety. That's what the wall is for after all, Dineh. Safety.

And elections, Sir.

People want to be safe.

And to get elected.

Elections? What are they to me, Dineh? Who can guess?

I'm not sure all the animals will fit, Sir, in a zoo. We're not talking about merely a few bats in the belfry, Mr. President. Are we?

I don't give a damn about any bats in any

belfry, Dineh! And neither does Myownia! So don't ask her! No more talking to Myownia!

I've never spoken with her, Sir.

And you never will!

Does she say much about any of this, Sir? The border? Immigrants?

Not to you she doesn't!

What about Myownia's family in her home country in Europe, Sir? Why did she Germanize her first and last name when she's not from Germany? Very curious new meanings she chose. Why did your own family Americanize your name from the German? Is there something you're not telling us about crossing borders, Sir? You and Myownia?

It's different for me and Myownia, Dineh. I'm not like other people. I have a right to do as I please. I can afford it.

That is indeed a great difference, Mr. President. If you don't mind my asking, how many of your wives where born overseas, Sir?

Who can keep track?! It's hard to keep track of things, Dineh! Things change so quickly. They live in this country now, Dineh. Far as I know. And they love it here. Love it.

Times are confusing, Mr. President. Studies show that more Mexicans have been returning to Mexico than entering the United States these past years.

There's the problem, Dineh! They come and go! Who can keep track! And that's why certain facts don't matter! Ask Press Secretary Bullcrap Baloney Bullshat! Stuff's always changing, and then you keep it changing, and who can keep up?! My enemies chase me, Dineh, but they can never keep up! The Mexicans, too, they are coming and going and going and coming, and taking my money with them! It's not only Mexico we're fighting on the border, Dineh. It's Guatemala! And whatever those other countries are called! And Texas! And the other states! Arizona! New Mexico! Goddamned California!

A lot of people, Sir!

Too many people, Dineh! And that is what has got to stop!

The people, Sir?

Who else?!

And there's all the animals, Mr. President. Plus birds. Fish. And what happens to the land and water when it too gets cut up and cut off?

There you go again with water, Dineh!

Sir, at least the birds and butterflies can fly over a high wall - most of them, not all - but we're talking hundreds of species of mammals, reptiles, and amphibians that will be trapped within a couple dozen miles of the border. Where do they find water? How do they eat? Seek shelter? Mate? Move? Live? Many are threatened, endangered, and currently under protection even before the wall.

At least they won't cross the border, Dineh! Not anymore! Or if they do, they won't get far!

Over the river and into the wall, Sir?

Exactly! Wait! What's this here on your twitter machine?! A jaguar! A giant wildcat caught on camera crossing the border! And it says that Tucson schoolchildren got together and named this big cat El Jefe! Ye Gods! Let's hope El Jefe has been apprehended, Dineh! This is what has got to stop! Who cannot understand the danger to us all?! Our southern border is being attacked! It is a threat to us all! El Jefe is stalking everyone! Schoolchildren! This is the most dangerous border in the world, Dineh!

That jaguar is amazing, Sir. Jaguars have a protected reserve in Arizona, but a wall would destroy the Jaguars' ability to reach it. Mexico, Mr. President, is not at the border with its army ready to invade. It's nothing remotely like that. You've got the US military bombing all over the world but what has Mexico done? You've got NATO guns and planes in Ukraine demonstrating within a stone's throw of Russian guns and planes. What happens if a mistake on that border sends everyone nuclear ballistic? There's nothing like that on the Tex-Mex border, Sir. You've got US warships demonstrating along the coast of North Korea, while North Korea could launch its artillery at any point and destroy Seoul, South Korea, a few miles away over that border, tens of millions of people in Seoul dead if attacked, even by mistake. What about that border, Sir? The US already totally destroyed North Korea once in the war, slaughtering hundreds of thousands, for what, Sir, anything? And how has that worked out for everyone? Or was that massacre for something, the Korean war? You can bet they don't call it the Korean War in Korea, Mr. President. What was it for

when the US slaughtered the Sioux and the
Apaches and all the other Native American
tribes, Sir? For land? Trade? Resources? Labor?
Isn't that what it was for, Mr. President? North
Korea rallied, with China backing it, and North
Korea - crazy as it was made to be - decided that
it won't be destroyed again. No matter what. Do
you really want to make an enemy of Mexico too?
North Korea has long had offers for peace and
some disarmament on the table, Sir, which every
US President simply ignores, preferring to
attempt to win by force, by starving them out. Is
this what you want to do to Mexico and to
Mexicans, Sir? Starve them out? And to Texans,
too, Mr. President? Texas and Mexico are huge
trading partners. Mexico is much closer than
North Korea, Mr. President, and much bigger.
And it has all of Central and South America
behind it. Do you want a DMZ on the Rio, Sir?
Wouldn't it be good to let the river and drylands
be? People in Texas and in the other
southwestern US states are already fighting
against the wall, Sir. Texans are mostly against it,
and most agree that the benefits of immigration
outweigh the negatives. It's as if people are
trying to tell you, Sir, in great big flashing lights:
No Wall! The border walls built there now are
cutting off precious water in the deserts and
drylands across hundreds of miles for many
species. Water, shelter, food, it gets walled off,
Mr. President.

Dineh, you're not Mexican are you?

Many of these species are in trouble, Sir. And

the border wall would carve through dozens more parks, refuges, fish hatcheries, and other protected wild lands, splitting them up. Plus tribal lands. Not to mention ranches, chopping through endless private lands. What about flooding and water flow in the river? You can't mess with that without violating treaty rights with Mexico. A wall, Mr. President, would destroy so much. People can get over, around, under, through a wall. People can trick a wall, Sir, and those walls will cause desperate migrants to try to cross in ever more risky ways, through ever more remote desert areas that kill. Animals can't trick a wall like that. It's the free living wildlife that you will be putting a stop to, Mr. President. That's all. And it's ugly, Sir. My apologies.

Are you half eagle, Dineh? Is that what you think you are? If so, you're welcome to fly back to wherever you flew in from.

Sir, my people have been around these lands for centuries. And even they themselves were immigrants, centuries before that. The world is full of migrants, Sir. Everyone, really.

Your people, Dineh? No! I won't hear it! You're one of us now! You're the chief bottle aide to the Ruler of the World! What matters most, Dineh, is whose side are you on! At this very moment!

A lot of Mexicans and former Mexicans are in Texas at this very moment, Sir. The Texas side is the side their lives are on. Isn't that what matters?

That's my point, Dineh! Texas is too damn close to Mexico for its own damn good! Texas is going south as we speak! We must chop Texas at the border to save ourselves! And as long as I've got the border, I might as well take the whole damn state, Dineh! I'll get the whole damn thing, put Texas in my pocket, and keep it there!

President Tyrump scowled at Dineh's handheld device then flung it high toward the Presidential Seal on the ceiling. Dineh lunged to catch it, rolling across the carpet.

You're quick as a cat, Dineh! A border wildcat! I better not catch you climbing that wall! You look like a lot of people we deport!

Dineh stood and came back to President Tyrump by his desk.

Mr. President, pardon me, but to me, you look like an immigrant in my land. My people have been here in this land so long that-

There you go again with your "people"! Dineh, you need to get over that!

And your wife Myownia immigrated to the USA only a few years ago, Mr. President. Wasn't there some question about her travel visa in the first place, before she got her green card?

My wife is strictly legal, Dineh! Strictly! Legal! How dare you! Myownia is a fine, proper, upstanding nude model! Like what the Ancient Greeks and Romans did, with their statues, a work of art, my Myownia. And perfectly legal! A perfect 10! Show me your visa, Dineh!

It's in my desk, Sir, not that I need one. My family has been in this land for so long they forget which millennium they arrived. Much longer than your family, Mr. President. People don't move without good reason, Sir. That's why I wonder: do you really think you ought to do it? Invade Texas? Do you really think it would go well for all concerned? For anyone, really?

It had better goddamn go good, Dineh, or there will be Hell to pay! And that Hell will be me! You want Hell? I'll give you Hell! Look at this tremendous document right here!

President Tyrump pulled a worn note out of his pants pocket.

Look right here, Dineh! My brilliant Press Secretary Bullcrap Baloney Bullshat authored this terrific work for me! We haven't shown it to anyone yet. One day, I'll tweet it! Justifications for the Invasion of Texas! Bullcrap's list of "Ten Bullets For Texas":

First Bullet: There are a lot of people of color in Texas! Many not US citizens! And many with little or no money! Texas is full of enemy types!

Second Bullet: Texas is a distant land, far from New York City and Washington DC! It was once a foreign land! No one likes a war fought at home!

Third Bullet: Many Texans speak a language other than English! They might be spies!

Fourth Bullet: Texas hoards huge reserves of oil and gas! Money literally flows out of the ground! Who can resist?!

Fifth Bullet: The military already knows where all the good targets are! Fireworks!

Sixth Bullet: Texas is full of women and

children! Easy pickings!

Seventh Bullet: Texas is empty inhospitable moonscape - or soon will be! Familiar fields of war!

Eighth Bullet: Odds are good that certain Texans wearing black cowboy hats and white hoodies will assist in the onslaught and policing! Texans love law and order!

Ninth Bullet: Well-placed Texan officials can be bought off! They already are!

Tenth Bullet: Recent opinion polls show that Texans by a healthy 2 to 1 margin prefer to be invaded and conquered than to be nuked off the map!

People think I'm only out to get Mexico and the border, Dineh! You and everyone else! Fooled you! Texas fits to a T all the criteria for achieving a glorious military conquest by the USA!

Yahoo! Google it! Get ready, Dineh! We're going to Texas!

President Tyrump crushed Secretary Bullcrap's PR list, then stuffed it back into his pants pocket.

Texas is a mighty big state, Sir.

And I'm a mighty big man, Dineh. I'm a charitable guy, you know. I'll throw any good people a few bones with the bombs and the bullets. As I see fit. The Texas War will do a lot of good, especially for me, and for the office of the Presidency, the way military conquests, invasions, bombings, and even mere saber-rattling work for any President of the USA. I'll be more popular than ever! So hold onto your cowboy hat and strap on your cowboy boots, Dineh! Yeehaw! We're going to war for Texas!

You don't think a Texas War might be taking things a bit far, Sir? How could it not all come to regret?

You can never go too far, Dineh. Not when you are the ruler of the world! My only wish is that the world was bigger. More to conquer! We already put down most of the rest of the world, so it's time to turn our attention back home. I'm a patriot! I love the homeland! After we take Texas, we'll attack Appalachia to control its coal, methane, timber! Timberrr!!!

Appalachia? Sir? You want to invade the mountains? Do you know how many guns people own in the mountains, Sir? It's probably one of the most heavily armed places on Earth. Like Texas.

Almost Heaven, Dineh! Why not attack Appalachia?! Coal is West Virginia! Coal is gold! Coal is there for ripping out of the hills! Mountain Mamma! So what if we have to nuke a few stubborn mountaintop holdouts?! West Virginians know about tearing off the tops of mountains! The better to strip the coal! And we won't stop in Appalachia!

I think the coal has already been spoken for, Sir. Long time passing.

Well I'm speaking for it now!

Solar energy, Mr. President? There are far more jobs and better jobs in solar energy than in coal. That's what all the studies show. There's more work there and better work, too, Sir. And the future as well. No black lung. No scorched Earth.

Work?! I don't have time for work, Dineh! How will I improve my golf game?! That's the only solar job I'm up for, sunning on the golf course. The sun has nothing on me. I'm the Sun King! Ask anyone. The more sun, the more heat in the world, the more I like it! Melting glaciers, rising sea levels, who cares?! It's fun to burn coal! It's fun to burn anything! I like it hot! Hot times!

"Thank God they cannot cut down the clouds!" That's what Thoreau said, Mr. President. Not even Thoreau could foresee the day the clouds would be cut down.

Oh, knock it off, Dineh, the sky is not falling. There will be many, many big clouds in your future, I promise. Who is this Thoreau anyway, and how much is he worth? What's a little rain in your life, Dineh? You mustn't worry unless I tell you to! Clouds will always be with us, big ones, thunder clouds, storm clouds - tornadoes! hurricanes! - you betcha! - clouds as far as the eye can see, I guarantee it! And whoever the hell Thoreau is, he sounds like an idiot to me. Probably makes his money in feathers. You need to stay away from those people, Dineh.

Feathers, Sir?

Lightweights, Dineh! Very light. All fluff. Nothing like me. I'm a heavyweight! I'm the heavyweight champion of the world! Look at me! I tell you this, Dineh, there's a lot more we can get from life! We can't let a few pointless clouds stand in our way! Cut them down, I say! To Hell with What's-his-name! What a Loser. Cut down the clouds! Let's feel the sun!

President Donbo King Tyrump made a fist and shook it in Dineh's face.

I want to invade the deep South to restructure its agricultural lands, Dineh! I vow to re-conquer the Native Southwest for its Native jewelry and crafts, and the many mines! I love turquoise, copper, and gold, don't you?!

Those are the four poorest regions in the USA, Mr. President, and you are talking about invading them all. Appalachia, the Deep South, the Native Southwest, the Tex-Mex border. Haven't they been through enough, Sir?

The four poor, no kidding? We'll fix them right up! No matter that they are neck in dirty neck in poverty after these many years of prosperity for all, no matter that they are overflowing with people of color: the blacks! the browns! the reds! except for Appalachia, a pity. The whites. Dirt poor or not, these sad realms in my country remain rich, rich, rich, rich in natural resources! How can we hold back?! I demand plunder! I mean profit! I mean prosperity! The prosperity that we so generously bestow upon foreign lands! Bombs and bullion! Missiles and money! Drones and debt! Dollars and...more debt!

I'm sure the people will be eternally grateful, Mr. President. Though at first they might flee. Or fight back. I mean there's a reason there are tens of millions of refugees running for their lives these days.

People love to move around, Dineh. Not that we can always let them. So many people are moving so many places now. I wonder why?

Bombs, Sir. Made in the USA. That's what a lot of people say.

Well, they probably deserve it! These people, they let terrorists live in their backyards! They grow them like weeds. Thank God, we've got walls for everyone!

First the bombs, then the walls, Sir? They say the bombs create the terrorists, Mr. President. Bombs breed terrorists. People don't like to be bombed, I guess.

Who says that, Dineh?

The scientists who study it.

You know, Dineh, you're lucky I like you. You're lucky you're so good with my little bottles. Where are those little bottles, anyhow?

Locked in your desk, Sir. It's not time yet. They are right there where they always are. Don't worry, I won't forget the code.

That's why you're my man, Dineh. You should relax and enjoy life. Bombs are often needed to make things work. To bring people to their right senses. If we didn't need bombs, we wouldn't use them. When we need bombs, Dineh, we use them. It's not that we like to bomb. It's that we have to. That's all. It's a need, a real need.

Do the migrants think so, Sir? Those who survive?

There you go thinking again! Don't do that, Dineh! Bombs and walls! Walls and bombs! It's a fit! It's the natural order of things!

One, and then the other, Sir. Where does it end?

It doesn't end, Dineh! It can't. We have too much invested! We have a bomb economy! You need to only be on the right side of the bombs and walls. It's beautiful that way, Dineh. The finances. How it all works. The mess is merely in the details. You know how it goes: Invade, Conquer, Privatize, Sell-off, Cashout, Repeat. Whatever the Banks want. What's good for the Banks is good for all! For all we know. What's good for the bombs is what's good for the banks! And vice versa! This is the way of the world, Dineh. Our military happily operates in most countries on Earth, and our National Security Agency happily operates in them all! Be happy as a banker, Dineh! I am!

I'm not a banker, Sir.

Happy as a clam then. I don't care. Be happy as a clam, and clam up! Your problems are not my problems, Dineh! Why does everything have to be my problem? I'm the ruler of the world, not a two dollar shrink! Keep your problems to yourself, Dineh!

Some people say, Sir, even US soldiers, that we have no business being in all these countries in the first place, and bombing them, Sir.

So stupid, Dineh. Business is the reason we go. You have to bomb people who, for some unknown reason, refuse to go along to get along, or to get along to go along - I forget how it goes!

The military, Mr. President, and the National

Security Agency are based and operate all throughout the USA too. Everywhere you look and everywhere you can't see, it's as if this land has become an occupied country, Mr. President. Some people say there is the One Percent and then there is everybody else.

Some people need to grow up, Dineh. Occupied?! Yes! By the illegal aliens! Otherwise, not at all! Preoccupied! Distracted. And rightly so! We have the greatest shows on earth right here in the USA the most powerful country on earth! And we have the best media when it covers me! Which it does a lot, since it knows where its bread is buttered! I'm gold, Dineh! Solid gold! I'm the greatest showman on earth! That's how you measure success. It all comes down to who puts on the biggest best show! Me! Brand Tyrump! I'm everywhere! In the world! Brand Tyrump rules all! Didn't some losers try to occupy Wall Street, Dineh?

The peoples' camp, Sir. They called themselves the ninety-nine percent, Mr. President.

And you saw what happened! Crushed 'em! Send in the police! Problem solved! Pretty simple, Dineh.

They changed the way a lot of people think about things, Sir. They changed the way people talk, what they say, what they demand. They identified the One Percent, put the spotlight on them, on vast inequality.

They are uncivilized! No good! Troublemakers! Trying to bring my country down!

And Occupy Wall Street basically wrote the presidential platform for Alle Peoples, Sir, and he almost beat Hilty Crimeton. The Democrats' One Percent stopped him. He would have been a tough out in the general election. Much tougher than Hilty Crimeton, Mr. President. All the polls showed it. The polls showed that we wouldn't be here today. The people preferred Peoples, Sir. The polls show they still do.

Goddamn it, Dineh! I won! I'm a winner! The past is the past. And the future is mine! I'll take care of Peoples! Alle Peoples be damned! Loser! Peoples is nothing to me! I hate Peoples! I'll stop him at the border!

Alle Peoples was born in this country, Sir. It was his parents who were the immigrants.

I'm talking about the border of the Presidency, Dineh! No way in Hell will Alle Peoples be allowed to cross that border! Now or ever! And in the meantime, I've got some border crossing myself to do. We're going all the way to Abilene, Dineh! Abilene or bust! And we don't bust, Dineh. I'm way too big to fail! I'm the USA! I'm Donbo King Tyrump! And I rule!

Why Abilene, Sir?

Who the Hell knows, Dineh! They probably have something worth something there! Cattle and oil! I imagine! They probably have a zoo, for animal huggers like you, Dineh. Texas is in Abilene. That's all I care about. And Texas will be mine! Then Appalachia! Then the Deep South! Then the whole Native Southwest! From sea to shining gold sea, Dineh!

It's not all roses though, is it, Sir? Where you invade and want to. Appalachians could be considered honorary people of color, Sir: the diabetes epidemic, drugs, and other diseases of poverty in Appalachia have darkened the color of many inhabitants' skin to a flushed red, or to a morbid splotchy yellow with greenish tinge. As it turns out, Appalachians are people of color too, Mr. President.

Great God, you are right, Dineh! Let's attack and invade them all! These people are the scum of the Earth! They are so very different from me it's as if they are not even of my own human species!: the Blacks, the Browns, the Reds, the dirty Whites, the hideous poor! Haters! Free-loaders! Carpers! Complainers! Useless Losers! Annoying! Obnoxious! Obscene! Nothing like me! Nothing to me! I will purify the country! All I need is their votes! And their dollars! To keep them in my debt! To push them deeper in! Or I can just sweep them away!

A living wage, Sir, a healthy wage might change everything, but the people don't have it. No guaranteed health care or college - what do you do? Turn to drugs? Suffer and die? Life expectancy is taking a hit, Mr. President. Many people are calling for a debt holiday, like in the long ago past, far before most people are led to remember, Sir. A debt jubilee. Debt forgiveness, Mr. President. Why not? So many people would benefit, the overwhelming majority. The banks don't need the money. They make up the money anyway. Or if they do need money, I'm sure you'll bail them out like President Obomba did a few years ago. You could take them over, Sir, the banks, if they start to implode, or even if they don't. And give the banks to the people, make them public banks, why not? Whose country is this anyway, Sir? Whose money? Let the people go, Mr. President. Free them of crushing debt. It would mean so much to so many. It would help the economy a lot. Isn't that what you care about, Sir? Debt jubilees have succeeded elsewhere, Mr. President.

How do you control people if you don't keep them in your debt, Dineh?! They're liable to do anything they want! And not what I want! And without the people's debt, I lose, I don't know, maybe a billion dollars right off the top! Who knows?! I need that extra billion dollars, Dineh, for my own self respect! And to maintain control! It's not possible to brainwash everybody like we do most people who get serious money and education, Dineh. For those who don't have the right education, or a big enough paycheck, it's hard to get them to do what you want if they are not sunk in debt! It's good to be brainwashed, Dineh! But it doesn't take with some people! I'm fortunate enough to be half brainwashed myself! At least I try to be! I like it! Works for me! Feels good! I scrub my noggin every night! I flip the varmint off my head and scrub my noggin till it gleams! Don't fight me, Dineh! Put your weapons down!

I'm unarmed, Sir.

Lucky for you. I always win. People need to get the right sort of education, Dineh. I have a book I can loan you, My New Order, the collected speeches of Adolf Hitler, a truly remarkable read. My ex-wife spilled the beans in an interview: I've kept it by my bedside. My New Order. You know my father got arrested at a KKK rally, right? It was in the papers. I love to make the papers! I'm German, you know, right?! German-American! And now fully American! No longer a dreary Dyrumpf, I am King Tyrump! Tyrump the Terrible!!! In America all things are possible, Dineh! I am the Czar of my own New World Order! Old wine! New bottles!

Whoa, Mr. President. Whoa!

What's wrong?! Don't worry, Dineh. We are not invading Russia during winter. Not this winter, at least. Much as I might like to. Their ruler, Vinomore Punchin, would find out, and that would bring trouble. Besides, Punchin is one of the whitest guys I know. Us great whites are almost an endangered species, Dineh! Of course, you wouldn't know how it feels to be endangered like we are. Make no mistake, Dineh: Vinomore Punchin is a great guy, almost as great as me, and he won't back down when you poke at his lands. Don't mess with Punchin, Dineh.

I wouldn't think of it, Sir. Who would?

Hilty Crimeton! That's who. What a great candidate she was! She scared people half to death with her war mongering against Russia. Russia! The other nuclear power! And then she goes and calls voters "deplorables"! Thank you,

Hilty Crimeton and bigshot Democrats, I owe my election to you! But they had better not ever try to collect on any debt from me! Thank God the Democrat bigshots did not let that damned Alle Peoples win the primary. That guy doesn't play fair. Who does he think he is, Santa Claus?! Free this! Free that! Education! Health care! Cheese!

Cheese, Sir? The free cheese program was started under President Reagan. One of your heroes, Mr. President.

Reagan was no Santa Claus, Dineh. Alle Peoples wants to be.

Better Santa Claus than the Grinch, Sir. That's what people say. People are funny that way.

Bah humbug! Fokkk the people! Fokkk Santa Claus! You can quote me, Dineh. Front page! On the cover! Filch them all! We took care of Hilty Crimeton. Alle Peoples, not so much. He tried to speak with everyone, to everyone! Strange guy. If push came to shove, you know, if the Demoskooks had nominated Alle Peoples for President to run against my fine self, then we might have had to, you know, kneecap him, I mean, needle him, I mean, maybe tease him a lot. That sort of thing.

I get what you're saying, Mr. President.

As for Russia and its leader Vinomore Punchin, we might prod that guy a bit, just for kicks and giggles, the media likes it, and the FBI and the CIA and the military love it - hey, bash Vinomore, scare the hell out of everyone, sell more weapons! - catnip to the corporate elite, my biggest backers - but I'm no Hilty Crimeton, I tell you that. How she could bray and blather unlike anyone at all! Always wanting to hammer and sickle Vinomore Punchin right in the gut. So unsophisticated. I can tee off on Vinomore on my Tyrump golf course, set him up in my Tyrump Tower, wine and dine him at my Tyrump resorts where we can do deals, carve up the world like in the old days when Vinomore and Russia had their own Great Wall to make money off of! God knows why they got rid of their wall, Dineh. Shows weak moral fiber, if you ask me. There are many ways to divvy up the lands but none more fun than buying people off! Of course, we'll bomb when we have to. China had a wall, Russia had a wall, and now, by God, the USA will have a wall! Press Secretary Bullcrap Baloney Bullshat can explain it all. The winners write history. He who bombs tells the tale! That's what I like about Texas, Dineh! Texas doesn't know its history!

Except how it does, Sir. Texas crushed its Freethinkers and Populists, Mr. President. Texas seems never to forget how to do that.

Sounds promising! I'll take your word for it, Dineh! That's what I like to hear! Texas understands only one thing: the power of the gun! Like a shot straight to the heart of Texas! Texas can't help it, so Texas can't help itself! Relax, Dineh. We are not invading Russia. At the moment. We are invading Texas! It's sunny in Texas. Texas winters are nothing. The Panhandle aside.

Imperial conquest, Mr. President. That's

what your critics say. They say that's all you think about. From sea to shining sea.

And from the Gulf, too, Dineh! The Gulf of Mexico, the Persian Gulf, the Gulf Coast, the gulf of my own mind! A lot of gulfs around the world! The US military goes gulfing like I go golfing! Golfing on the gulf! I am my own best critic, Dineh, you know that. Anyway, I am the only one worth listening to, the only one I can hear. To Hell with the rest. What else can be done? The bankers love war! It fills the vaults!

And the graveyards, Sir.

Business is business, Dineh. In the Beginning there was Business. And in the End...

Bombs? Why drop the biggest bombs on the poorest countries, Sir? Bombs for the poor, Mr. President? What about the law, Sir?

Fokkk the law, Dineh! I am the law! We are talking Texas here! Texans love guns! And fences! What is the wall but a big beautiful fence with guns backing it like the teeth of a shark?! Guns are good, guns solve problems, guns are what make this country great! And gates! Big fences! To protect our Texas gold: gas and oil! Texas gold, gates, and guns! Texans love these things! Texans love Texas!

Mr. President, Sir, Texas is officially a part of the USA. Texas remains legally unavailable for invasion.

Who have you been talking to, Dineh? Reality is whatever we make it out to be, not what you think it is. Legality is a state of mind! My mind, Dineh! Reality is whatever the top two advisors in my electoral campaign claim it to be for me. You know Bannin Banbart Bannem and Connie Con Conwar. It was their idea to conquer Texas ASAP! Conwar and Bannem are my shock troop advisors! They brought me to power and I trust they'll keep me here, Dineh. It's not as easy as it looks! In every election a majority of the wealthiest voters in the USA vote for my party, the Republican Party, but their votes only go so far, even when we grease the scales! I have to get some lower income votes too: that's where Conwar and Bannem come in. They know how to do it. They know how to go all folksy, jokesy, silly, pokesy. They know how to act gruff and buff, to bluff and stuff. You got to get down and act like you know the town and can clown around and be against the brown! You got to get grandpa and grandma out again and again to vote against their grandkids! That's the only way, Dineh!

You're the living proof, Sir!

It was a close call, Dineh. If grandma and grandpa had sat this one out, I would have got clobbered, even with most of the white males and most of the rich in my pocket like every year. And Hilty Crimeton would have got thumped too by Alle Peoples. Thank God for Medicare! Who knew, Dineh?! Medicare saved grandpa and grandma and they saved me! That's why I can't cut Medicare even though I want that money for myself! After grandma and grandpa...the deluge! The deluge, Dineh! That's a lot of water, Dineh. You can appreciate that!

Climate collapse, Sir? The end of the world?

Socialism, Dineh! The real end of the world! Sure I need to shove Conwar and Bannem back into their cages half the time - you can't sic gaping fang people like them on the world every day and night, night and day, Dineh. Too much screen time and reapers like those two tend to scare the hell out of people, in the wrong way! Who could sleep with Bannem and Conwar always on the loose?! Not even me with my special nasal inhalers! But whenever the time is right, I unlock the cages and out they race, Bannem and Conwar, chomping and slashing left and right, right and left. Freaking out grandma and grandpa and the other true believers and gullibles, chasing them right, hard right into the voting booths. Bannem and Conwar, they'll go after anyone and anything to bury the opposition! Wild and ruthless and focused! Like a bullet to the brain, a bomb to the butt! That's how you win, Dineh, that's how I won, using Bannem and Conwar to bash and crush anyone who would oppose me! Bannem knows that pure white makes pure right makes pure might. Conwar knows that reality is whatever you make it! Reality is like make-believe except for real! Conwar and Bannem, better than anyone, know the right alt realities to suit my needs to a Tyrumpian T! Tyrump! Conwar, Bannem! Together we are a match made in the eternal bonfires of cash! Dineh, imagine how rich and powerful I can be! A majority of white male voters has not voted for a Democrat for

President since Lyndon Johnson, a Texan, Goddammit! Way back when, Vietnam War. Then we cranked up the brainwashing. Big time. We had too. People were starting to get uppity - even the white people! They were getting ideas, Dineh, thinking they could control the money and all, as if they imagined it might be their money, their country, their way of life! It's not their money, it's not their country, it's not their way of life, and it never will be! Random people don't own this country. I own it. The people never did. I do! It's my money and my country, and I would brand it all Tyrump! If I could! And if I can get all the bombs to fall in all the right ways and all the right places, maybe I will own it all, at long last! My country! My world! Right and wrong! Tyrump!

But Texas, Sir? The Texas? Land of the Free? Home of the Brave? Do you really think you can conquer Texas, Mr. President?

Texas?! Dineh, is that an American name? It sounds Native to me! Not American at all! Texas illegally broke from Mexico! Illegal immigrants from the USA - can you imagine? - moved into Texas and helped overthrow the Mexican government, which only goes to show: illegal immigrants are a menace everywhere for everyone! Holy Shia, we thought the Muslims were bad. Texans can't be trusted to control all that oil and gas, unlawful infidels of The Badlands. They sure as hell don't know what to do with the border! They just live there! The USA can't be running around privatizing only Muslim lands, Dineh. The Muslims keep knocking our heads off in their home countries! It's as if the Muslims themselves want to control all the oil and gas where they live. Why should they, when our guns, planes, ships, and bombs are bigger?! Meanwhile, our original enemy lives closer to home: in outlaw Texas! Scoundrels everywhere! These crafty Texans want to pump their own oil and gas themselves! And they want to keep all the sunny and warm land too! Who do they think they are?! They want to keep it right there in Texas the way they like it! That doesn't seem fair to me, Dineh. Others would like to help and have some of the oil, gas, land, and weather. I know I would.

It's a travesty, Sir. Hard to comprehend.

There's no shame in helping yourself, Dineh. That's how the cat gets fed.

I see, Sir. Which cat would that be, Mr. President, the wildcats on the border?

The big cat on the block, Dineh!

What about the blowback, Sir? My people have a saying...

Your people? Goddamn it, Dineh! Americans are your people! Americans have a saying too, and if I could remember what it was... Don't mess with Texas! No, wait. Long live the King! That's close but not quite it. Well, no matter, whatever we say here in our land, it is great! You can take that to the bank, Dineh. I'm not attacking you, Dineh, don't worry. I'm attacking Texas and Texans! This is not history repeating itself, I assure you. This is history as sequel. So what if the USA was out of control back in the day? Technicalities, Dineh. Today we are a state strictly endowed with law and order. I am in charge! Back then we were baboons, monkeys throwing shit. Not today! Back in the day, the USA was wild! Illegal! We were Conquistadors, a nation founded as Empire! Manifest Destiny! We were slavers! Exterminators of Natives! We outgrew that. Long ago. Today we are civilized. Today our destiny is made in a different way. We control the money, the web, and the arms trade. We watch football. We use plastic. We Instafacetwit. Even in Texas! We have armed the land, the air, the seas, and space from Houston to El Paso. From the bottom of the oceans to the top of the moon, we've got weapons systems lined up and on alert all around the universe! And Texans can't be trusted! They keep too much oil and gas to themselves, too much river and border land, too many fossil fuel pipelines, and far more than their fair share of our beautiful weather! The fact is that the state of Texas was and remains a legal fiction! The existence of Texas is a monstrosity of the law! Texas is no lawful part of our world! Texas is no more an original part of the USA than the USA is a province of China! Tell me no! Texas must be severed and reattached!

I will not tell you no, Sir. No, Sir.

You're goddamned right you won't! I am the President of the USA! I am the law. I am Sovereign. I make the law by who I am and by how I act. I know what legal is. It is what I do. I am nothing if not totally goddamned legal!

You are totally goddamned legal, Sir. And Texas?

Texas is illegal! I do not care what the United Nations says! Texas does not belong to the UN! Texas belongs to me! If I need to bomb the UN, then I'll bomb the UN! And Texas!

The United Nations is in your home state, Sir. New York. The Empire State. You don't want to bomb your home city and state, do you, Mr. President? There's a bad precedent for that, Sir: 9-11. The second one.

Don't I know it, Dineh! New York, New York is the United Nations Headquarters. Don't forget! Never forget! Too close to Wall Street for comfort! We can cut its power, raise its rent, evict it if the UN interferes with my conquest of Texas. I will see it destroyed brick by brick! Entire teams of executing officers know exactly what to do with rogue groups like the UN, Dineh. All I need to do is tweet.

Don't do it, Sir. Put your twitter machine down, Sir.

President Tyrump tweeted: Dinnay needs to grow up, Pronto!

President Tyrump put his handheld back on the presidential desk.

Thank you, Sir. I appreciate that, Mr. President.

You need to put first things first, Dineh. Stuff is about to get real.

Now hold on, Mr. President, can the state of Texas possibly be a threat to the USA? How is

Mexico a threat? Mexicans are just people, Sir.

In what state is there no serious challenge to the right of the Winners to rule, Dineh? We have to blame someone for the crappy jobs, the crumbling roads, the polluted environment, the crowded schools! Let's blame, Texas! Why not?! It's so close to Mexico! We have to blame somebody to keep everyone from blaming the One Percent, as the Losers call us. That's what they call me and my kind, Dineh, the One Percent. So, okie-dokie. I will too. They say the One Percent are to blame for bad pay, crap jobs, no health care, no jobs, poor schools, pricey education, broken bridges, toxic lands, dirty water, smelly air. They say the One Percent are evil! What they forget, Dineh, is that the One Percent supports the ninety-nine percent who are total Losers. Total. Losers. And Mexico needs to do what it is told. I have to blame somebody, otherwise people will blame me! Of course I can't use that kind of language on the campaign trail. The One Percent do not like to be talked about that way. The One Percent do not want to be talked about at all. The One Percent do not want to be known to exist. But the election is over, Dineh. I won. The One Percent will do what I say, because I am the One Percent of the One Percent. I am the mouth and the muscle and the means. Don't doubt me. So what if the One Percent run this country into the ground?! It's their right, because it's their country!

Of course, Mr. President. However, can you make Texas look truly outlaw enough to warrant an invasion? People like Texas. Texans likes Texas. Remember, Mr. President, people in Texas voted for you.

Only the Whites, Dineh. Loyal to their blood, I suppose. Hellfire and Damnation! People in Texas voted against me too! No matter. Enough people would have voted for me, if they could have, in Iraq and Afghanistan and Libya and Syria and Yemen and Yoohah and Yoohee and everywhere else we've been bombing, invading, conquering, and blessing with the rule of the God Almighty Dollar. People around the globe would love to vote for me! Some of them. The right people. They support me. Texas supports me. The owners of this country will cheer for every invasion I announce! The One Percent is my base. Them and the local yokels. The loco local yokels! I love the loco yokels! They truly understand me. They love me too! We're big, bad, and beautiful together! And most of all, Beautiful!

Mr. President, polls show that people think you were elected in a totally shameless manner. Calls for impeachment, cries of "Shameless!" are everywhere. There are protests in the streets, Sir. In every city in the country.

The protesters are pathetic, Dineh. And the impeachers are a bunch of rotten fruits. We ignore them like we always do, and we smash them as need be. What are the police for if not to guard every square foot that we own? That's what the police need to do, keep people in their proper place. So what if I embrace and extol my inner Shamelessness? That's what great leaders do! Shamelessness runs for President from both parties every time. It's a no-brainer. Who actually gets elected? Saints or sinners? Angels or Evil? The wise or the wiseguys? Prey or predators? The tender or the tough? We all know the answer: The Bankers! The Owners! The Financial Fearsome! The One Percent. The source of stupendous shamelessness! I merely make it more fun than before. That's what low brain energy people fear: My kind of fun! I'm funny! I'm the One Percent of the One Percent, I have very high brain energy! Very high.

A lot of people don't find you very funny, Sir. My apologies.

A lot of people are stupid, Dineh. Oh, I know the One Percent are scared. They are scared of me and the debtors both. The One Percent Banker Owners - the Bowners! - they pretend to democratically manage the corporate empires. The great con. I don't know who it's fooling, really. The Bowners own the political parties and set up the electoral system to select One Percent Bowner frauds, I mean fronts, for their interests rather than for the interests of the ninety-nine. This does not happen by accident, Dineh. Only one political party is allowed power - the One Percent Bowner Party - which has two wings, the Republican Bowners and the Democrat Bowners. These are private parties with private interests - the One Percent! They cover themselves with public promises like plastic fig leaves. Two wings of the same firebreathing dragon! What a staggering illusion of choice!

People are afraid of dragons, Mr. President.

Cheer up, Dineh! It's carnival! An electoral extravaganza! A bright big Corporate Day parade! A firebreathing dragon balloon! I'm all over the News! The Videos! The Snaps! And the Chats! I am Twitter! I'm on all the Shows! I'm the Face of Facebook! I'm so big, Dineh, I don't even know how big! I can't see the end of me! Who can?! I'm all profit all the time! I'm the Star of Stars! I'm everywhere in an Instant! I know you think I'm crazy, Dineh. Admit it. You think that beneath the spectacle lies a special kind of insanity.

No, Sir. Well-

Careful, Dineh. Be Careful.

I mean, Sir. I do not think you are crazy. I know-

No, no, no, Dineh. You can think whatever you want, as long as you do what you must. You know how it works.

I suppose so, Sir.

I'll tell you anyway: the Republican Bowners pump up the true believers like militant toy balloons. They use white male supremacist pathologies as hot air, while the Democrat Bowners blow hard upon the rest: pathetic women and angry minorities and desperate children flapping pathetically for whatever uplift they can get. Worker white males! Women and children and people of color! All indebted and owned by the Bowners! Next election, I'm tempted to switch parties and run as a Democrat Bowner - wouldn't that blow their minds! What's the difference?! The voters are not the point! It's the Bowners' election! The Bowners project shameless glorious images of themselves above the carnival crowd, like marvelous brand name drones! I am the greatest Bowner brand of them all! Brand Tyrump! For the voters it's all carnival all the time, miserable phony carnival that it is. Hail Tyrump! Vote Tyrump! The Bowners? What are they to me? They cannot afford to be too stupid.

They need you.

Who doesn't? Wishful thinking is for Losers! Long live the carnival! We all live in the Funhouse now, Dineh!

Or is it a Haunted House, Sir?

No! It's the White House!

The big house.

It's not the outhouse, Dineh! This is the Inhouse. I'm so In I'm everywhere. Don't worry. Shameless debates and shameless elections and all the chest thumping about gender and race and guns and God and who is more militaristic and more devout than thou.... This is what sells! Forget who owns your sorry ass! When the people are pitted one against another, the rule of the Banker Owners goes unchallenged! Democracy has no chance in this system, Dineh. I can't take the credit. The shameless fix was in long before I one-upped the vote. It could be worse!

How is that, Sir?

Hilty Crimeton could have won! And then she would get all the money that should rightfully go to me! I know some people say this country was founded upon Empire, can you imagine?! Extermination of natives! Slavery for blacks! Forced migration! Conquest over a continent! Over two continents! Three! Four! So what if this is who we were?! I am a new brand! Brand new! Brand Tyrump! The new operating system, update XXX! The Empire never sleeps! Hell, it never puts its guns down. Why do you think the National Security Agency spies on everyone all the time? Ours is a system of checks and imbalances against the debtors! A dollar democracy for the One Percent, of the One Percent, by the One Percent. Drones and debts for the rest. It's so rich!

People see your blunt talk as shameless, Mr. President. It's upsetting. You lose approval even of the One Percent.

Sue me! Everyone else has. I don't want approval, Dineh, I want power! Guess what? I got it! The more I fuss, the more I bluster, the more crazy fun I have with my enemies and potential enemies - and who is not a potential enemy, Dineh? - the less the Bowners can predict what I will do! Who knows how I might be most shameless next?! Maybe I'll go crazy on behalf of the poor rather than on behalf of the rich. Fat chance, but the Bowners can't know that because they don't own me like they own all the other politicians. Even if they think they do! Buy and sell, bought and sold, silver and gold! The One Percent care only about their bank accounts! They want me to do what is good for their rule.

They want me to stump for their shameless asses, in shameless debates, shameless elections, by shameless divides. It's a farce run by the Bowners, hyped by the Bowner media, lapped up by true believers and by those who have had their eyes put out. I am the Lord of the One Percent of the One Percent! Of course I'm shameless! And smarter too. Look at me! I'm so smart I scare myself! I kill the killers! I outshark the sharks! I smash the smashers! It's in my pure Aryan blood, Dineh! What can I say, I'm a big owner. A Bowner! From way back. The best! Tyrump! As President I might as well be God. Go USA! I call the shots. What I say damn well goes. If I say we invade Texas, then we damn well invade Texas! You better goddamn believe we do! Don't tell me who supports me and who is a goddamned fool. There is no shame in power. I outshamed my opponents. I won, fair by foul. I am fully endowed by the Oval Office to act as I see fit!

Even in invasion, Sir? Of Texas? Your lawyers may balk at this one. No legal right to invade, et cetera.

Total crap! Who cares what lawyers say? I can buy extra legal opinions to satisfy the Petty Bettys. If I say the invasion goes, the invasion damn well goes! I need that border land, Dineh, we Bowners need the whole damn state to build the Great Wall of Texas, to make a profit, to keep power! To stay on all the shows! To be in every device! To get in your brain and to stay there. To own it all, to own everyone, to own you!

Everyone wants to be owned, Dineh! When we own you, we own your wallets and pocketbooks, we own all your accounts! We own what you think you own! We own what you think! We can sell you, trade you, buy you, cash you in and cashout as need be. We tap you in, we tap you out. Ring you up, ring you out, power you on, power you off. It's all about power, Dineh. Cash in to cashout. Be always cashing. Cash me if you can. We all know who gets the money, Dineh.

Texas might object, Sir. It might go Native.

Over my dead body! Don't doubt me, Dineh. The One Percent are mad for more money! For more control! For more greatness! Texas will have to pony up. What good is immense power, if you don't fokkking use it?! Texas is mine!

Dineh put one hand to his forehead, the other to his heart. The power of the Presidency gushed through his being, that disembodied adrenal surge coursing through boardrooms and offices, swirling around conference tables, flooding airports, rushing across the metal wilderness, lighting up the silicon universe, warping through fiber optics, magnetic in waves, screaming into enormous vaults of money, and shrieking into the loaded chambers of guns and bombs, in, out, down, up, around, shaking all about, power, power, power, pulsing from broker to agent, agent to General, General to CEO, CEO to President to banker and back, exploding through every realm of rule.

Dineh saw debtors scattered everywhere, fragments, shards after a great blast, tiny specks, molecules, atoms, particles, gone, nowhere, never more, once was, not ever.

In that moment, Dineh could see every bit of existence, humans, animals, plants, planet Earth, even somehow the solar system, galaxy, universe for what it once might have been. Alive. Awake. Aware.

Alive.

Dineh looked and listened ever more closely.

He saw skeletons. Burnt flesh. He saw blood. Brains out of skulls. He saw a planet ripped in half.

And then he saw his own skeleton walk into the room. It walked toward him.

The skeleton grinned. Its bones glowed.

We need serious action, Dineh said finally to the President.

Our greatness depends on it! cried the President. Let America be my America again!

Dineh stared past the President.

Mr. President, I know exactly what you mean. I know what must be done.

Don't think, Dineh. Act! Thinking never gets you anywhere. Thinking is for Losers. Do not be a Loser, Dineh!

Your logic, Sir, it is unimpeachable. Your words are absolute. No matter Congress.

Now you're talking, Dineh! You're speaking my language at last!

President Donbo King Tyrump thumped the map of Texas with his fist.

Call the Generals! I want them in here now!

The President did not have long to wait. The

Generals were already in the know: three dozen intelligence agencies had recorded every word.

Here come the cops! joked President Tyrump. Dineh, put your hands up!

Dineh did not raise his hands, at which point he was tasered and knocked to the floor by the Secret Service. Dineh struggled to breathe as he lay crumpled against the base of the wall.

The Generals awkwardly confronted the President standing in a semi-circle around his desk in the Oval Office.

The Chief of Staff of the Army stepped forward to speak for the others:

We've come to fix this, Mr. President. Taking the border was one thing. But by God, Sir, you don't mess with the rest of Texas. Not on my watch, Sir.

The Army Chief held out a pair of handcuffs and tried to capture the President.

President Tyrump grabbed the handcuffs and flung them across the room. The handcuffs bounced off the face of a portrait of President Tyrump, one of many images of himself that he had ordered hung upon the wall.

What I say goes, General! Have you no shame?! Is there no justice?! Are you insane?! Who will save the White men?!

The White House, you mean! Who will save the White House?! I side with you, my President! declared the Commandant of the Marine Corps. He punched the Chief of Staff of the Army. Teeth flew. The ensuing brawl left all the Generals lying on the floor.

At this point, the Chief Executing Officer of Goldun Sichos investment bank entered the room flanked by the Secretary of the Treasury (a former Goldun Sichos executing officer) and the Director of the National Security Agency. Numerous other Banker Owners from the government and the corporate elite crowded into the Oval Office.

Boys, said the CEO of Goldun Sichos to the Generals on the floor. Get up.

The Generals stood and saluted Pittance Viper, CEO of Goldun Sichos, who did not return their salute.

Mr. President, said CEO Viper. Proceed. You call the shots as you see fit, as we selected you to do. These good men - he inspected the Generals with a flat flick of his eyes - will bother you no more. They will do as you say. You have the support of the entire country and indeed of the world. He nodded to the officials in suits and ties.

A prominent Pastor stepped forth and blessed the proceedings.

The Army Chief picked up his teeth and slipped them into a pocket.

We good folks need to stick together, declared President Donbo King Tyrump.

I will be more direct, said CEO Pittance Viper: Finance must be feared. Or simply obeyed. The debtors must fall in line, and they will. Now go spiel them once more, President Tyrump. Do your little song and dance. Go boast to the good debtors about power and...what's that other thing? Freedom! Or whatever you might call it.

Remind them of the needs and blessings of power, our power. Do speak in their hokie jokie way, whatever works. We know that you will say the Right Thing, President Tyrump.

Let's go kill some Texans! shouted President Donbo King Tyrump.

Wait, what? said the Marine Commandant.

Too late, said Dineh, pushing himself up from the floor. Then the mob of officials trampled him down again.

First they came for the wretched of the Earth, said Dineh to the hardwood, and then they came for the Texans.

Say what? said the Marine Commandant, overhearing Dineh. We are fighting for the wretched of the Earth?

You are fighting for the One Percent, Jarhead.

Semper Fi! shouted the Marine.

Get moving! ordered the Commander of the Air Force, pushing the Marine Commandant out of the Oval Office.

The Invasion of Texas was on.

Dineh went missing. A report filtered back to Washington DC of his being glimpsed in the desert Southwest riding a horse into Mexico. At the border, the CIA drone lost sight of him among a sea of women, children, people of color, and others fleeing for their lives. Amid the dazzle and glory, the excitement and thrill of The Invasion of Texas, no one gave the disappearance of Dineh further thought.

Except for the President.

President Donbo King Tyrump was pissed. He ordered that the entire northern border of Mexico be "carpet bombed into oblivion!" The President considered, not for the first time, bombing all of Central and South America, giving them the North Korea, Vietnam, Thailand, Laos, Cambodia, Iraq, Afghanistan, Pakistan, Sudan, Somalia, Libya, Syria, Yemen, etc, etc, etc treatment so that there be no refuge for anyone anywhere.

What Wall Street's economic hit men had not yet destroyed, Washington DC's bombs and bullets would finish off. There would be crisis and then there would be capitalism to reap the whirlwind. Millions would suffer, millions would die, a relative few would profit. The way of the world.

The President of the USA punched the air.

I am who I am! President Tyrump called to reporters upon touching down in his helicopter near a slaughterfield. I make my America great again! This is everything we ever wanted! We own the world! We own all! God bless the USA! Where else can a person rise from mere billions to go out and conquer the planet?!

Thus did fall once again the exploding hammer of American Exceptionalism on Mexico and on the Americas, Central and South, as it continued to fall on the world abroad - Asia, Africa, even Europe - and at home: Texas, Appalachia, the Deep South, the Native Southwest, the corroded cities and blighted suburbs and poisoned countryside.

A series of hurricanes raged from the Atlantic Ocean and the Gulf of Mexico, killing many refugees, climate change with a vengeance.

I cry havoc and let slip the dogs of war! screamed President Tyrump to the grateful corporate media who lapped it up and broadcast far and wide, day and night, around the planet, around the clock. The Banker Owners demand plunder, profit, power, as do I, President Tyrump! My patriotic religious supporters long for Rapture, and so I preach: If all goes nuclear we will ascend to Heaven and laugh at our enemies in their Hell on Earth! The killers will drown in their own blood! Is that shameless? It is Rapturous! It is the way of Power. The Right Way. I once heard somewhere, I forget where, that the Navajos go by the Beauty Way. And the Bowners by the Supremacist way! We might as well tell it plain now while we are in the thick of the fight! The banks above all! He who lives by the mighty dollar, profits by the mighty dollar! By the War Way, the Military Way, the Capitalist Way! He who lives by the Sword, prospers by the Sword! In War we are most alive, in War we are most free, in War we are most powerful, in War we are most rich, in War-

At that moment, a giant hand swooped from the sky and grabbed the President.

It might have been the terminal hand of Climate Change. It might have been the terminal hand of a malfunctioning computer system, or of a hacked one, signaling a real or false nuclear attack - who could tell? It might have been the

Hand of God. It might have been the impulsive whisk of any number of gods.

The hand swiped President Tyrump off the presidential podium, popped him up to the clouds, and launched him into literal orbit around Earth.

The President's flight path intersected with a US military satellite guiding missiles and drones in deadly endeavors. The President's body exploded upon the satellite. The space weapon malfunctioned. Missiles and drones were re-directed from the targets to their original sources.

A multitude of other weapons were similarly unleashed.

Thus ended the spectacular Invasion of Texas.

Thus ended the glorious rule of President Donbo King Tyrump.

Thus did the eternal results of the most recent shameless election come in.

There was nothing left to do but to pick up the pieces.

If any were to be found.

II.

"Robber! Thief!" cried President Hilty Crimeton from sleep. Upon waking, she shouted, "Dineh!"

Presidential Aide Dineh moved quickly from his desk to President Crimeton who floundered up to a sitting position on a couch in the Oval Office. "A terrible dream! Horrible! A nightmare!

I dreamed that Donbo King Tyrump won the Presidency and not me!"

"Are you sure you actually won?" asked Dineh.

"I won all right," said President Crimeton. "You joker, Dineh. More people voted for me than for Tyrump. But now I've had this horrible dream, a nightmare! President Donbo King Tyrump won the Presidency, and then he invaded Texas...and he blew up the world!"

"Texas?" Dineh asked. "Our Texas?"

"The one and only, Dineh. I was robbed! Twice over! Robbed of the Presidency and robbed of my chance to become a billionaire before I die!"

"How evil!" said Dineh.

"Oh you were a horrible person in my nightmare, Dineh! You were Tyrump's aide and you did not care about money at all! In the end, he tried to kill you!"

"For not caring about money?"

"You would think, right? No! For disloyalty to his insane plans! Oh thank God I won the election, but sometimes it is too much. I need a thick stack of thousand dollar bills to calm me down, Dineh. Go get me some serious money, right now."

Dineh glanced at the liquor cabinet on his way to the Money Closet. The cabinet appeared untouched. As for the Money Closet, a converted office filled with hidden safes and filing cabinets stuffed with cash and jewels, Dineh was the only person in the world who possessed the quintuple key and password access codes needed to get past the alarms, lasers, locks, and other martial and cyber deterrents to the wealth depository set up at the order of President Hilty Crimeton. Not even President Crimeton could access her Money Closet without the assistance of Dineh. She had never made time in her busy schedule to learn how.

Now, one might ask, why would the top elected official of the richest, most powerful nation on Earth require the installation of a large Money Closet across the hall from the Oval Office, next to the secret server through which she communicated privately, that is, in secret? A) Because she liked money? B) Because she loved money? C) Because she worshiped money? or D) All of the Above.

Dineh knew his was not to wonder, merely to find his place and to hew within it.

Still, it was obvious enough. President Hilty Crimeton loved money. And then some. For spiritual emergencies during moments when Dineh might not be around, President Crimeton hid currency of large denominations around the White House, as well as in her private homes under cushions, behind pictures, upon shelves, and in assorted drawers, cabinets, and books, also in her pantsuit. Hilty Crimeton took great pride in cleverly hiding her cash from the cleaning crews and all workers.

Returning from the Money Closet, Dineh handed small banded stacks of large bills totaling several hundred thousand dollars to President

Crimeton, which she received with a great heave of relief. She stroked the bills, ruffled the edges, eyed the denominations carefully. She pressed them to her heart. "Thank you, Dineh, this helps wonderfully, you have no idea."

"My aim is to serve, Ms. President."

"A proper aim, Dineh," said President Crimeton. "For you."

"Yes, Ma'am. This has been a very busy start of the week for you already, and you've come out of your nap early. Maybe we should reschedule the remainder of your appointments."

"To hell with that, Dineh, there's money to be made! What good is being President of the United States of America if you're not getting rich along the way?! What do people think I'm in this for?! The honor? The glory? Hell no! The moolah! I'm not here for my health, Dineh. Shot that to pieces years ago. My marriage is a disaster - effed up from the start. My husband? Ye gods! Sick rapist, don't quote me. My daughter? At least she's set. Married rich like I raised her to do. And Dineh, all this shit we have to deal with: health care! women's issues! child care! living wages! new jobs! elder care! prisoners and prisons! For God's sake, Dineh, who gives a shat about prisoners, there are so many of them! And more all the time! We are the greatest country in the world, Dineh! An exceptional people! The most exceptional! Unique in all history! And we have the most prisoners to prove it! Whatever happened to the good old days?: 'Take no prisoners'! 'Hang 'em high'! Nowadays, all everyone talks about is their rights! How is anyone supposed to get rich?!"

And with that, Dineh dropped over dead.

His time was done. Or so it felt.

Rousing himself slowly after fainting, he looked up to see President Hilty Crimeton glaring imperiously down at him.

"What on Earth is wrong with you, Dineh?!" said President Crimeton. "There's money to be made!"

Dineh stared into President Crimeton's spinning right eye. "It's going to be a long few years," he said. "If we make it."

"Of course we'll make it!" cried Hilty Crimeton, perched firmly on the Oval Office couch. "I'm the President of the USA! How could we possibly not make it?! Who would dream otherwise?"

Dineh plummeted again into dark.

CHAPTER TWO

Death by Dynasty

*P*residential Aide Dineh woke on the floor of the Oval Office where President Hilty Crimeton was kicking him in the ribs with the metallic point of her shoe. "Get up, Dineh! Get up! There's no time! There's money to be made!"

Half conscious, moving from one nightmare to another, Dineh croaked, "I'll pay! I'll pay!"

In Dineh's one nightmare, President Crimeton accused him of stealing money from her Money Closet. In his other nightmare, she was pounding him with the torturous toe of her shoe.

The reality was complex. In fact, Dineh *was* stealing money from President Crimeton's Closet. He wasn't stealing some of it. He was stealing all of it. Dineh was the central smuggler moving cash from the One Percent into the accounts of the Peoples' Revolutionary Front. Dineh and the PRF were liberating this money, not stealing it, from their point of view.

The Peoples' Revolutionary Front invested the money in progressive movements for social change across the US and worldwide. The PRF also liberated counterfeit money that the US government was constantly seizing to put out of circulation. The PRF recycled it into President Crimeton's Money Closet where Dineh layered thin rows of real money over the mass of counterfeit. Assorted other revolutionaries of the PRF had lifted this real money from members of the One Percent, nationally and internationally, who would be most embarrassed to be associated closely with President Hilty Crimeton. In this way, every last dollar in President Crimeton's Money Closet had been liberated or was fraudulent.

"I'll pay, I'll pay!" said Dineh one last time before coming fully awake and attempting to block the blows of President Hilty Crimeton's shoe.

"You're goddamn right you'll pay!" cried President Crimeton. "You're paying right now!" President Crimeton kicked Dineh again.

Dineh crawled away from the Oval Office couch and the metal toe of the outraged President.

"How dare you pass out on the job! No one works that hard around here, Dineh, except for me! I'm no slave driver! I'm a slave to Empire myself, to Dynasty, to Destiny!"

"And to the People?" said Dineh. He managed a sitting position on the floor.

"Oh, to hell with the People, Dineh. You know that. Save it for campaign season when we need a few wishy-washy votes. It's time to get down to real politics here."

"Brain-washy votes is what you'll need come election season," said Dineh. "I don't know if you can get them."

"We got them, Dineh. How could you forget?! It wasn't easy. You hit your head when you fell. There was nothing I could do to break your fall, Dineh. Believe me. I'm trying to establish a dynasty here, and you're flopping around on the floor like...like some goddamn thing flopping around on the floor!"

"I'm sorry, Ms. President. The campaign has destroyed my nerves. I don't know how we won. It's a terrible burden you carry. You have a nation to lead. A world to protect. A planet to heal." Dineh rubbed his ribs.

"Lead, protect, heal? That's good for election season, Dineh, not for life. I don't 'lead' the world, I command it. I don't 'protect' the country. I defend it, aggressively: I attack to get rich and richer. I don't 'heal' the planet. I run it into the goddamn ground, if I want to! It is my Dominion! That's right, Dineh. Nation, country, land of the free, to hell with that, I am the Ruler of the World! We're in it for the money, are we not?! I'm no billionaire yet, Dineh, if you can believe such a horrible thing, not like that awful Donbo King Tyrump. I'll be worth more than that cheap huckster soon: you can bank on it. Winner take all! I deserve it! More than anyone I know, I ought to be the richest person in the world. The President of the United States of America deserves as much. We are the most powerful country on the planet, the richest! Dineh, get off the floor!"

Against his better judgment, Dineh extended his hand to President Hilty Crimeton seeking a bit of help up.

"What the hell are you doing, Dineh?! Do I look like the hired help around here? Get your ass off the floor, pronto!"

"I think my ribs are broken."

"Is that my problem? You cover that up. You tripped and fell against the coffee table, or my desk, or the fighter-bomber statue, or whatever. Don't push me, Dineh. You know what I'm capable of." Hilty Crimeton cackled. "I made Donbo Tyrump look like a little shrimp of a wimp during the campaign. We all saw it. I may not have his cash in pocket, today, but I will before long, I promise you that. In the meantime, there's this." She gestured to the fighter-bomber statue. "The USA has the biggest military in the world by far, with gun installations and martial operations in the vast majority of countries on Earth. And I am in charge of it now. You had better believe I'll get my money. I've already gotten a Hell of a lot of it. We'll have war with Russia yet! If all goes well. Over my dead body we won't!"

"The world looks to you for leadership, Ms. President," said Dineh. He hauled himself onto a chair.

"The world must fear me and my power, Dineh!"

"Oh, they do. We all do."

"Don't I know it! If not me as dollar leader, who? Someone else, that's who! Why should I not gain and possess as much money as possible? Why not all of it?! Sure I know, some people think they are entitled when they are not, but some of us actually do carry the entitled gene, Dineh. We have it naturally and then go on to earn it more! We know we are the most deserving. We grew our entitlement on our own, yes we did! Maybe we weren't born with all of it, maybe we were. We get stronger as we go. We are naturally powerful! Money is the only way to be sure of anything in this godforsaken world! Why do you come to work in the morning, Dineh? For the money!"

"I do appreciate getting paid, Ms. President."

"I would think you would be grateful! It's pure money that makes the world go merrily round. Without money, this life is for nothing. Look at all I've sacrificed!"

Dineh thought for a moment. "It's true. You've done things that most of the rest of us would not remotely dream of doing."

"We can't all be billionaires, Dineh."

"So it would seem."

"Dineh, don't be daft. You have your place. And I have mine. People need to learn what their proper place is, first in life. How could I possibly speak for everyone, even as President? Universal this and universal that: health care! living wages! rights and more rights! Who can keep up?! There's always something more! People make nothing but unreasonable demands! First and foremost, I need to speak for myself as President! Think of it. Have you ever seen anyone more deserving, more truly prepared, more put together than I am? Anyone more practical and professional? I've earned my Me Time as President, have I not? Am I not the most powerful President of the USA?! This is all I've lived for! Who is my equal now, Dineh? You tell me. Am I not the greatest President you ever knew? Oh, who cares. I will certainly be the richest! You can bank on it, Dineh. Bank on that. You can bank on me, Dineh."

"Oh, I do, Ms. President. Believe me."

President Crimeton laughed, in that delirious rich way of hers. "I don't believe anyone, Dineh. Why would I? Have you met my husband? No, Dineh, I go along to get along! You can bank on it!" President Crimeton laughed and laughed. She didn't mean to be scary. She meant the opposite. Miscalculations made Hilty Crimeton who she was. She didn't mean her laughter to sound dollar-intoxicated and dollar-supremacist. It would be too generous to say that her timing was off. Her laughter was not exactly of glee, although it might pass for such, and was meant to. A skeptic might hear in the President's laughter something unusually braggadocios and salacious, pornographic of power, something belligerent and phony, and something nuts. To a skeptic, the president might appear to be a grade B actor in an even lower grade movie. Dineh heard something more, he heard hatred and contempt. And that was partly why it felt good to liberate the money taken by the One Percent, to give it back to the people, for use by the people.

"Dineh, thank you, I appreciate all that you do for me. I appreciate your loyalty and your confidence, your trust in me and my powers, Dineh. I appreciate you very much, Dineh. You know I do."

Dineh rubbed his ribs. "We have traveled to the ends of the Earth together, Ms. President."

"We go where the money is! Who would open the Money Closet for me, if not you, Dineh?"

Dineh cautioned: "If push comes to shove, the National Security Agency might be able break in there."

President Hilty Crimeton narrowed her eyes. "Yes, well we would know if the NSA did try to break in there, now wouldn't we...?"

"We would know, I'm certain. I did what you told me, Ms. President. Certain hackers..."

"...computer experts..."

"...who need protection..."

"...a modest reprieve..."

"...from the Justice Department...."

"...my employees...."

"...have leverage against the NSA."

"...to protect me."

"Your dollars..."

"...my finances..."

"...need protection..."

"...ironclad..."

"...even from the NSA..."

"...especially from the NSA, Dineh! Of course. Keep your enemies close or kill them - that's my motto - like that Gaddafi in Libya. When he tried to use his gold to set up an independent currency in Africa, the French President and the British Prime Minister and I made sure Gaddafi's day was done. Gaddafi had dirt on the French President, so, too bad for Gaddafi. That's how I succeed in life. I go with the flow, you know: the flow of power. You do good work, Dineh, when you're not fooling around on the floor. Don't skip meals, Dineh. I certainly don't, and look where it has gotten me." President Crimeton stroked her pantsuit.

"That must have been what went wrong," said Dineh. "Maybe I don't get enough rest. We chase so many dollars around here. And those bills don't make it into your closet by magic, Ms. President."

"Look, Dineh, we all want what is best for the financial system, don't we? And what is best for the financial system is what is best for me and vice versa, and what is best for the financial system and for me is what is best for the country, it must be. This is all that anyone can know with any certainty, or, shall we say, with ample plausible deniability, Dineh. Sure I understand I am no Donbo King Tyrump, not yet. But I will surpass him, Dineh, him and all the rest! The Saudis! The Chinese! The Russians! The Germans! The English! The Dutch! My God, the Dutch East India Company is the gift that keeps on giving. Oh to be a slaver back in the day! Wait? What? Who said that?"

"Who said what, Ms. President?"

"Precisely. Thank you, Dineh. Just checking. You have my eternal gratitude for your profound loyalty." President Hilty Crimeton put a hand to her head suddenly. "Oh and...and oh...my..."

President Crimeton sat down heavily on the couch.

She swayed, slumped, jerked, rocked, then keeled over upon the edge of the couch and slipped off thumping onto the floor.

Dineh barely managed to catch the President's head, preventing another concussion as she had suffered during a previous incident when he had not been close by.

Dineh knew what to do.

He and Hilty Crimeton had been here before. He was well trained by now.

Dineh took the nasal spray bottle from his pants pocket and prepared to aid the President.

He hesitated.

He considered how would he make it through the day without having his ribs attended to. He wondered if he should do it. It was so tempting, a quick spray to the nose, a little dose. He imagined it might knock his head off, though the pain in his side would vanish, merely a dull remembrance of things gone by.

Somehow he couldn't do it.

Maybe he was weak, maybe he was strong, who knew anymore? Dineh muttered unpleasantries to himself.

Then he focused again on President Hilty Crimeton. He administered two quick doses to her nostrils. He thought to ask for an increase in his salary.

President Crimeton's eyes flung open. "I feel

good," she said. She sat up, bracing her hands on the floor. From there, Dineh helped President Crimeton onto the couch again. "Oh, yes, much better now. I feel like myself again."

Hilty Crimeton stood up. She walked around the couch.

"One of these days, Dineh, you are going to tell me what exactly is in that little bottle of yours."

"Oh, it's..."

"No, don't tell me now! Wait till I retire and complete my memoirs. Whatever it is, keep it coming."

"You can ask your doctor," said Dineh. "Your doctor prescribes. I merely administer."

It was liquid cocaine. The doctor had told Dineh so that Dineh would know to go easy with it for the necessary Presidential applications. It was an old-fashioned remedy, the doctor admitted, but highly effective in the case of Hilty Crimeton.

"Are you sure you don't want to rest today, Ms. President?" asked Dineh, rubbing his ribs.

"And lose an investment? Not on your life!" President Hilty Crimeton flexed her arms above her head. She rubbed her nose. She took a deep breath and exhaled fully. She shook her head. "You are one of us now, you know that, don't you, Dineh? You have put your shoulder to the Captain's wheel here in the capital. You are an honorary ruler of the world."

"A higher compliment from you I do not expect to receive, Ms. President. I do my best. As do you."

"Let's not be sappy, Dineh. We need to get those executives and officials rolling in here! And keep that little bottle handy. I have my dynasty to build and to protect and to build the more! To hell with legacy, Dineh. It's dynasty that I care about. What does the military call it? An Army of One! Join us, soldiers, be an Army of One! Build our dynasty for us! Empire is such a clumsy word. I am a Dynasty of One, Dineh! Now let's book some funders. Line them up. Send them in. We are open for business!"

"Wide open, Ms. President."

President Crimeton cackled. "You and I, Dineh, together, we will fill the Oval Office with all the loot in the world!"

"As you wish, Ms. President." Dineh glanced at the appointment book. "You've got Saudis scheduled this week, some Israelis, a couple Englishmen, two officials from the Netherlands and Germany, and of course more of the usual Wall Street crowd. Some, not many from Africa and South America, and a lone individual who claims to hail from Russia and China both. All have donated to the Crimeton Foundation for the Greater Gold. And we expect these financiers to also carry on person cold cash for the Crimeton Foundation, which we will secure in the Money Closet. Quite promising hours and days ahead, Ms. President."

"Who is the richest appointee, Dineh? I hope you had the foresight to schedule him first of the week."

"We are talking mere hundreds of millions of dollars difference with most of this crowd. I mean, a German, an Englishman, a Saudi ... it sounds like a bad joke, but those three appear to be neck and neck in wealth and investability. I did in fact schedule them first. Of course, you have your weekly Financial Update meeting before then. And the Vice President has requested five minutes of face time this morning. I did him the courtesy of scheduling him in."

"Vice President Fonie Fleece, what a total tool," said President Hilty Crimeton. "What can I say, we needed someone to balance the ticket one way or another, I don't remember. It seemed important at the time. The truly important thing is that he thinks like me and is obedient. The bad thing is that he thinks like me. He thinks he's as good as me, and as entitled as I am. He only wants my money."

"Vice President Fleece is quite wealthy already, Ms. President."

"Of course, Dineh. How could he not be? You don't get near me without being absolutely loaded. Don't be silly. Most members of Congress too are millionaires, which is as it should be."

"I wonder then, Ms. President, if we might discuss my salary-"

"Some other time, Dineh." President Crimeton pressed the banded stacks of large bills to her cheeks. "I'm feeling better now."

"Yes, Ma'am."

President Crimeton kissed the currency. She stroked it. She reluctantly returned the money to

Dineh. "For safe keeping," she said.

Dineh wrapped the bills in fine cloth. "Of course, Ms. President. Very safe."

"Wait, Dineh! The first appointment..."

"The Financial Update?"

"Who is scheduled for the FU meeting? He-Whom-We-Must-Not-Despise?"

"That would be Chief Executing Officer Pittance Viper of Goldun Sichos investment bank."

"Exactly! That reptile! He's our reptile, Dineh. Our golden reptile. Get him in here. Wait!"

"Ms. President?"

"To hell with the Oval Office, Dineh. It stifles me. So many people come in wanting to talk politics. It's not really what they have on their minds. Why do we keep the money so far away from the Oval Office?"

"It's merely across the hall."

"Too far. Let's meet Mr. Viper today in the Money Closet."

"Inside it?"

"It's a former office, Dineh. The Money Closet! Where the money is! Goldun Sichos has nothing on us! At least they shouldn't. Goldun Sichos' home turf is our home turf, it should be, and they need to know this now more than ever. I want to meet CEO Pitt Viper with the jewels and the bills and the gold and the coins."

"As you wish, Ms. President."

"It only makes sense, cents, and more cents to meet Pittance in the money pit where we can show off. We also have the big bucks to throw around. Oh, and, Dineh, grab the fighter-bomber statue from the Oval Office. Put it on a money cabinet. Pittance will get the point. He knows where his billions and trillions come from. We'll remind him. Some fools would call this the art of the deal, Dineh. I call it power politics, when I'm feeling polite. When I'm feeling mildly salty, I call it Thug Diplomacy. That's how you handle reptiles, Dineh. You have to show them who is the bigger thug."

"It takes a visionary to be President, I've always said. As you wish, Ms. President, I will move the attack plane into the Money Closet in preparation for the FU meeting. Has the stature of the national dollar ever looked better, Ms. President?"

"Now you're talking my language, Dineh! Get Viper in here fast. Let's show him where to stash his cash, park his bills, drop his change, put his dough! Send him right in. The Money Closet awaits my hospitality and his financial exuberance. I feel a billion dollar smile coming on, Dineh. Maybe two billion. Maybe more. Maybe a trillion!" President Crimeton winked and gave a thumbs up.

II.

"Dineh!"

Not long into the meeting, wild screams echoed from the Money Closet.

A laser bumped and activated? The

President seared?

Dineh heard bizarre notes of joy mixed in with the shrieks.

Happy screams, Dineh realized, among the happiest he had ever heard from President Hilty Crimeton.

"Dineh! Come in! Sit down! Close the door!"

Carefully, using the arm opposite his injured ribs, Dineh picked up a folding chair and ventured into the Money Closet. He shut the door and sat triangular to the two heads of Empire, President Hilty Crimeton, ruler of a political dynasty, and CEO Pittance Viper, head of a financial dynasty. President Crimeton sat on a padded seat by the fighter-bomber statue, while CEO Pittance Viper sat on a hard wooden bench, shoved against a cabinet full of tens of dozens of millions of dollars in cash.

"Don't look at me that way, Dineh," said President Crimeton. "I offered him my seat, but he insisted, saying the President should have the seat of honor. Pittance Viper! What a gentleman!"

CEO Pittance Viper smiled at Dineh in the way that he always smiled, apparently toothless. Where teeth might have been gleamed instead what looked like bone.

President Crimeton's glittery eyes were as wide and excited as Dineh had ever seen. "Dineh, we finally did it! We did it! I finally did. It will be done. My will be done! At long last, Dineh!"

Dineh slipped unconsciously...maybe it was the lack of sleep, maybe it was the pain in his ribs that caused his mind to skip into absurd fantasy, even as an enormous sinkhole in his guts opened so powerfully he felt disemboweled. Crazy thoughts flashed through his mind:

Universal health care?

Debt relief and financial protection for all?

Ample living wages?

Guaranteed jobs and income?

Free education through college?

Green energy investment?

All out efforts against climate change?

Nuclear abolition?

Abolition of state homicide?

Massive prison reform?

Prison abolition?

The end of insane drug policies?

The end of military conquest?

No more arming space?

Wholesale nationalization of crushing industries and banks?

Affordable housing?

Free child care?

A shorter workweek?

Paid vacation time and parental leave to match other nations?

No more profiteering of any kind?

Huge new investments in infrastructure and green space and public transportation and public schools and housing for the homeless and workers and in medical research and healthy affordable necessities like foods, organic agriculture, clean water, clean air, and...

Goldun Sichos CEO Pittance Viper stared at

Dineh as if Dineh had sprouted three heads, green horns, razor scales, and inflamed bug eyes.

"Are you insane?" hissed Pitt Viper.

Dineh had spoken aloud.

President Crimeton cackled. "Dineh, you knocked your head! You are too funny, Dineh! You choke me senseless with your joking!" For long moments, the President's laughter seemed to come at the expense of her breathing. "That's why I keep him around, Pittance. He's as sharp as my collection of vintage bayonets. Dineh knows we are gathered privately here, not publicly." Hilty Crimeton pattered smoothly, victoriously, like General Peacock after a war. "He knows we save the Hoo-Haw for the Yoo-Yaws. It's not time again to shoot down all those irresponsible pipe dreams. I'm the President of the USA, the CEO of the World, my job is to conduct private business behind public fig leaves. This is the only setup that works the way things are supposed to work. The Democratic Party is private, the Republican Party is private, the Commission on Presidential Debates is a private corporation, for the greater good of all! In this country, we have private issues and we have public issues. We are focusing here in my Money Closet on private issues. Normally we do this in the Oval Office but today is special, I can feel it. I'm getting richer than ever today. Dineh you know well how things work. The Election is over. We will turn to public issues once again at the proper time, in a few years at the next election. I don't know why they hold those things so often. It will be here before we know it. For now, Dineh, focus!"

"Of course, Madame President, I don't know what I was thinking, even in jest. You were so excited, I lost my mind. I'm sorry. I keep waking in the middle of the night thinking we are about to get trounced by our primary opponent, Alle Peoples, let alone Donbo Tyrump in the general. These things are all that Alle Peoples talked about. And he almost got us."

"Forget Peoples, Dineh. We knifed Alle good. He never had a chance, you know. He got lucky and made it look close for awhile, and then he met his brutal and richly deserved reckoning for all his talk of free college, living wages, free health care, jobs for all, saving the planet, and spanking the banks. We had a harder time with Donbo Tyrump, as you know. Talk about close! Apology accepted, Dineh. Better hold your tongue in the future. Viper here has a weak heart and can withstand only so many shocks to the system. CEO Pittance Viper is accustomed to the golden treatment, Dineh, first, foremost, and finally."

"Of course, Ms. President. My apologies. And to you, Mr. Viper."

"Dineh, look!" President Crimeton shoved an object at Dineh's face. "Look, Dineh, look!"

"What is it?"

"Look at it! Look at what Pitt Viper gave me! A coin purse!"

The purse was brown. It was small, flat, could easily slide into a pocket. President Crimeton stroked in slow repetition its smooth brown material.

"It's Puerto Rican."

"A coin purse?" said Dineh. "Do they make those anymore? For coins?"

"You're missing the bigger picture, Dineh. This purse can hold credit cards, folded bills, IDs, badges, bonds, bar codes - entire bank accounts, Dineh - and, yes, a few coins. And it's *Puerto Rican*. Take it. Look."

Dineh assumed that CEO Viper had slipped a gold coin of large denomination inside. He took the purse from the outstretched hand of the President. It was made of leather, an unusual thin, very fine leather. The quality was remarkable and must have been worth a fortune in itself. Unfortunately, the purse was disappointingly empty. "Very nice," said Dineh. "A bit light."

"It's not light, it's brown. You don't get it," said the President, shaking her head. "It's the purse itself. The material."

"I admire it," said Dineh. "It's very delicate."

"It's skin."

"Calf skin?" Dineh assumed, though now it was beginning to dawn on him that it might be the calf skin of some exotic animal, possibly an endangered species. Maybe the skin of an Asian Elephant calf, or the skin of an Amur Tiger cub, or of an African Wild Dog, or - then Dineh began to grow nervous - possibly the skin of a Western Lowland Gorilla infant. He guessed each aloud.

"Warmer, you're getting very warm," said President Crimeton with an excited fierce gaze.

And then Dineh dropped the money purse onto the Money Closet floor.

At first, he could not bring himself to say it.

"Puerto Rican skin," he whispered.

"Bingo!" said the President.

"We have a winner!" declared CEO Viper.

President Hilty Crimeton slapped the money cabinets behind her with the flat of her hands. She leaned over and picked up the money purse.

"Thank you so much, Pittance! And Puerto Rico thanks you."

"My pleasure," said Pittance Viper.

"Dineh, how many Native American tribes are left in the USA?"

Stunned, Dineh eventually responded, "Oh...I don't think that would be..."

"Just kidding, Dineh! A little payback for your silly campaign promises joke." President Crimeton stroked in slow repetition the human money purse. "Dineh, I am ecstatic today to meet with this fine gentlemen, Mr. Pittance Viper! Do you know why? He's the man with the cash, is he not? He's the top bankster. Banker, sure. Mr. Viper is a fine gentleman, Dineh. He is the man with the cash who controls and directs the other men - and occasional woman! - with the cash. Mr. Viper is an upstanding American, the finest, representing the gold standard of US and global financial institutions, Goldun Sichos investment bank. And he is here today to tell me something very important. Namely that the Saudis are not the Saudis, the English are not the English, the Japanese are not the Japanese, and the Germans and Dutch and the rest are not the Germans and Dutch and the rest."

"From where did you get the Puerto Rican skin?" asked Dineh.

"From Puerto Rico, beautiful island! What President Crimeton is taking great delight in explaining to you, Dineh, is that I am here today as Chairman and CEO of Goldun Sichos investment bank to represent an international consortium of investors - mostly European, North American, and Asian Oilan, plus Japanese, the honorary whites. Money knows no ethnicity, no border, no boundary."

"The usual crowd," said President Crimeton. "Any Russian? Chinese money this time? Or are they out of bounds, Pitt?"

"No bounds, no bound!" said CEO Viper. He sat very straight-backed and upright against a Money Closet cabinet.

"Well, Pittance ... politically speaking ... Russia and China..." President Crimeton and CEO Viper exchanged an awkward look. "We can't speak about it publicly. Not even in private."

"The skin..." said Dineh.

"There are no bounds," said CEO Viper.

"He means..."

"She means..."

"I mean..."

"We mean...the thing is, finance cannot tolerate borders and boundaries, certainly not of the monetary sort. Nor the political. Profits cannot abide it. Dollars are preeminent."

"Where did the skin come from?" asked

Dineh.

"No borders, really?" said President Crimeton. "Where will the deal take place?"

"In Puerto Rico."

"Within its borders?"

"That's where it *begins*," said CEO Viper.

President Hilty Crimeton clapped her hands and rubbed her palms. "Puerto Rico will be the puerto of departure, so to speak. They don't call it the Rich Port for nothing." President Crimeton held up the coin purse and shook it in Dineh's face.

"Once upon a time, it was rich, maybe," said CEO Viper, "but Puerto Rico is bankrupt today and deep in debt. A pity."

"The Christopher Columbus effect, I suppose," Dineh muttered.

"I'm sure he did all he could," said President Crimeton. "Just like those good people in the South, back in the day."

"Christopher Columbus! A great negotiator!" cried CEO Pittance Viper. "One of my favorite people in history! Chris Columbus, a man who knew what he wanted, and took it all! 1492. More than half a millennium of conquest. And centuries more to go!"

"Profit, Viper," corrected President Crimeton, "not conquest."

"Hilty, always being political. So politically correct," said Pitt Viper. "Profit not pillage. That is so diplomatic of you. It takes a pillager to be a CEO."

"It's my job to be diplomatic, Pittance. Profit.

Free market. Democracy. Debt service. These terms are all interchangeable with pillager, I know as well as you. Pillage or be pillaged, what can you do? However, not everyone thinks that way, which is why we have to be careful what we say. It's good to speak freely in the closet here, but one must take care not to form bad verbal habits that may find light in public. Lucky for you, Viper, Puerto Rico sounds much more appealing than Puerto Deuda. Port of Debt, Debt Port - it's just not that catchy. Am I not right, Dineh?"

"How can it be legal to use human skin?"

"The deal is what it is, Dineh. It may be legal someday soon. If not, no matter, right, Pitt? There's the unofficial economy and the underground economy both. Pick your poison. There's more than one way that the world is ruled, Dineh. There's more than one way to make a profit in international economics. Honestly, Dineh, do you think we send the Army, Navy, Air Force, Marines blasting all over the world out of the goodness of our hearts? Or out of fear? Fear is for the loyal consumers, the loyal debtors, not for us rulers. Big guns and little guns, they all bring a big return on investment. What's good for big bombs is what's good for big business. Hell, big bombs is big business! Do you know how many guns, bombs, drones, planes, tanks, and other weapons of war this nation sells throughout the world each year? We're by far number one in war sales! This nation conducts military operations and sometimes all-out conquests in 98 percent of the countries on earth! We've swayed elections and overthrown governments in half or more of the countries of the world! Our greatness knows no bounds! We don't do it because we are afraid, Dineh! We do it for the moolah! You want to talk economy?! The gun economy is a big one. It's not the oil and gas economy, but what is? Sometimes even we great investors are forced to dabble in mere skin purses around the edges, in ports tropical and otherwise."

"Naturally, we own the island of Puerto Rico now," said CEO Viper, "if there was ever any doubt before. The banks own it, on behalf of the people of course, and on behalf of this country, and myself. Now more than ever, technically, we own it. Lock, stock, and smoking gun barrel over the barrel, the banks own Puerto Rico, and for that matter most of the US and much of the world. US Corporations control about half the world economy, about the same as after World War II, still today. It's only natural, like gravity, sunlight, and, well, banks! Our Practical Policy for Puerto Rico is perfect for times like these," declared CEO Pittance Viper.

"What Practical Policy?" asked Dineh. "Another one?"

"Oh, really, Pittance?" said President Crimeton. "If your Practical Policy idea is not so very new, then why are you willing to deal me in today so very generously? Why this grand gift of a Puerto Rican coin purse? Times being what they are."

"Does the purse have a name?" asked Dineh.

"For precisely that reason, Hilty. 'Times being what they are.' What are they?: Uber Aware. It's the internet age. Everyone knows everything now. We can't hide nearly as much for nearly as long as we once could. Emergency measures are required. That hacker journalist fiend, Justice Assured of Wikilooks, and that cyber traitor Forward Showem, the NSA leaker in Russia with his girl, and that Army wannabe whistleblower Shallsee Manifest in prison where she belongs, and..."

"In other words, the only thing holding back the rabble from you and the banks, CEO Viper, is me," said President Crimeton. "Only the power of the Presidency can protect your King Midas life."

"A full return on our investment, that's what we expect from you, President Crimeton. We invest in you and your career, you invest in us and ours. You do your job, Hilty, we do ours. You represent one wing of the Business Party, and we banks are business writ large. We mean business. We have much business to mean."

President Crimeton leaned over and high-fived CEO Viper.

"How many purses are there?" asked Dineh.

"What more can Wall Street extract from Puerto Rico?" said President Hilty Crimeton. "Isn't the wealth mostly gone?"

"High finance is a wonderful thing, like magic really," said Pittance Viper. "We can make money where none exists, out of nothing, thin air, *ex nihilo*. It's what banks do. I had thought of naming my firstborn son Ex Nihilo but my wife threatened divorce."

"Which would have been costly," said President Crimeton.

"Especially in my case. Understand: banks don't loan real and existing money. Certainly my banks don't. Nor do our competitors' banks. Instead, we create debt for people by putting digital deposits in accounts when we extend a loan. Then we receive payments of interest, and hopefully payment of the principal eventually, even though we never had the money of the loan in the first place. Oh sure, we control a lot of money not created *ex nihilo*, but we loan vast sums from out of nowhere. We collect whatever interest and principal we can. If the debtor defaults, we sue and collect whatever we might, and simply write off losses. Poof! Never existed squared. They aren't real losses. The loaned money never existed anywhere but in the digital sphere of our made-up records. Don't tell me that make-believe isn't powerful. What a business! Of course we don't let the debtors know this. The few that do uncover the reality can't do anything about it. We own Congress, the Presidency, and the Judiciary having bought them all, directly and indirectly, and having worked other levers of social power to control what people think and do and know and believe. If the people really knew how the system runs, there would be a revolution. We can't have that. We would crush it, but they would try. It could be messy. The people would want a digital holiday from the make-believe, a debt holiday, debt abolition even. The people all know that something is wrong, but most don't know exactly what even if they think they do. They have hare-brained theories, which we stoke and supply from the background. That's where you come in, Hilty: you protect us, day in and day out, all in the guise of democracy. You are our shield. You make the make-believe real, almost human. You put a face on it. That's how it works. Money from nothing. Politics from nowhere. You know how it is. Why would anyone want to be anything other than a banker?! Or a banker's loyal helper?! To Hell with that damned Alle Peoples running around saying, 'The business model of Wall Street is fraud!' Well, maybe it is, maybe it isn't, depends how you look at it, but you don't *say* it. So we had to put a stop to him and his pathetic run for President. The business model of Wall Street is Power! The political model of Washington DC is Power through Business! Corporate Power! Of, by, and for the Corporate Elite! The fraction of a percent that owns the world and rules the world!"

"And war," said Dineh.

"Excuse me?"

"The business model of Wall Street, the political model of Washington DC is power through war."

"When necessary, Chief," said Viper. "War too."

"You mean always. The US is bombing in multiple countries as we speak. It's constantly at war. And always somewhere other than here. Except for the occasional 9-11 retaliation."

"Yes, Dineh, war. War too," said CEO Viper. "That's how you get this system working in the first place, and then protect and extend it in the second. Well, it takes a lot of good, hard work to pull this off. Sometimes we don't write down enough bad dollars from our accounts, we exaggerate our wealth, and that's when we get in trouble. You can't invest in other financial institutions and vehicles doing too much of the same thing. That's how you go bankrupt, when one ship goes down they all go down. If too many investors who have loaned to each other too much of this fictional web of currency try to pull too much money out all at once, then, boom! we all go bust."

"Until bailed out by the taxpayers," noted Dineh.

"Precisely. That's what the previous great President Bars Bomba Obomba did for us, bailed us out with the people's money, many times over and again. Oh, Democracy! It's wonderful!"

"Sounds like Bankocracy to me," said Dineh.

"Bankocracy! Brilliant!" said Goldun Sichos CEO Pittance Viper. "Unfortunately, it doesn't poll well. Not at all. But that Obomba...we've never seen another like him. A most glorious service he performed for us. We had our pants down around our ankles, broke as could be, in a way the whole nation could see. Obomba could have spanked us hard. He could have given those dozens of trillions of dollars to the people, direct into the economy, instead of to us. He could have kicked our broke asses to the curb and over the curb to rot by the freeway. He could have nationalized more than one giant bank and industry. We think he wanted to, a little bit. But he saved us instead. And he was gracious enough to kill the public option for health care, which would have put our pals in health insurance out to pasture. And our good friends the Republicans in Congress didn't help Obomba either. They shot down a bigger infrastructure stimulus package to the states. No matter! President Bars Bomba Obomba pulled our pants back up for us with a great big smile on his face! He even tucked in our shirts! And straightened our ties! So that we looked presentable again. Such a good man that gracious Bars Bomba Obomba. Oh sure, sometimes he shot off his mouth too much at us, and we were forced to give him a cooler. We subsequently refused to attend his meetings and threatened to withhold future campaign contributions when he started getting pissy about the big bonuses we began handing out to one another again. Well, we made sure he got the point right away, not to go bad-mouthing us too much, and then he toned down his words, instantly. That was why we put him in power in the first place, he had the two great features any good President needs: he obeyed the banks, and the people liked him! Be assured, we did not fail to appreciate his precarious political position when he badmouthed us that one time, though we would have moved Heaven and Earth to take him out of power entirely if he had kept it up. Politicians need to keep their popularity ratings from tanking totally to zero, but you should only go so far when criticizing power. There are other ways: flash your skin, your gender, your smile, your fancy wallet!"

"Your coin purse!" said Hilty Crimeton.

"Appeal to people's hopes and fears, and bigotry and ignorance. Whatever works, we don't care. So long as you don't criticize power much, so much that people might actually begin to think they can act on the criticism. Fortunately, honest Liberals are the most brainwashed people alive, while honest Conservatives are the most ignorant. We know what works to keep everybody in line. The honest progressives, let alone socialists, they simply need to be crushed. Hey, it's us or them. And it will always be us. We bank on it, do we not? One of us must go extinct, the socialists or the bankers. Not the bankers, obviously."

"I learned a lot from President Obomba," said President Crimeton. "That is, from you, Pitt."

"We are all learning a lot here," said Dineh. He stared at the coin purse.

"On to Puerto Rico!" said CEO Pittance Viper.

"To squeeze dollars from sand!" said President Hilty Crimeton.

"And flesh," said Dineh.

President Crimeton crumpled the purse in a fist and raised it before her. "And skin, blood, and bone! The benefit to the economy will be incredible!"

"And to you, Ms. President."

"This is only the half of it, Dineh. The idea is to contract private flesh stations, Pitt tells me, where people can go to sell their blood, have patches of skin removed from their bodies, and even donate bone marrow, and extra strips of tendons and ligaments, plus teeth, and duplicate or partial organs. All for cash in hand!"

"Nothing ex nihilo for them," said Dineh.

"Of course not. Our whole system would collapse, our banks, everything," said President Crimeton. "What's good for the select few is not good for the masses. But for the masses: Out of work? Unable to buy necessities? Problem solved! Body up! CEO Viper says, You can do it! *Body Up!*® is being considered as a trademark name for the flesh stations if we can get this thing through Congress: *Body Up!*® I like it!"

"What doesn't kill you makes you money," said CEO Viper. "That's the free market. It's a win-win for bankers and corporations both, tapping directly into the mainline of flesh and blood commodity possibilities. We work people hard for our gold, as they would work us, if they were in our official offices."

"Which they never are."

"One can't be too careful, Dineh. Think of our consortium of investors ... not only Wall Street but the several other Wall Streets of the world in Canada ... Britain ... Germany ... France ... China ... Hong Kong ... Japan ... Switzerland ... but in this case, Euro-American investors primarily. As well as Saudis and other Oilans. Even Russians. And a few others. The whole world depends on what we do. In better times, we make a lot of money simply by loaning the federal government funds through our central bank, The Federal Reserve. We control it, though the government created it and makes some appointments and could dissolve it, but we basically get what we want - after all, we pay a lot for the electoral campaigns, so US Presidents tend to do as we say. We loan the government money by buying Treasury bonds with money we make up out of thin air. Then government eventually pays back all of this make-believe money, with interest! It could not be more beautiful."

"If the government would establish its own bank, then there would be no need to borrow from you private bankers. Then there would be no flesh stations," said Dineh.

"Dineh has a point, Pitt," said President Crimeton. "A national bank would cut you banksters down to size in a hurry. It's totally absurd that the US government has to borrow money from the private banks through the Federal Reserve - named that way to fool the people into thinking it's a government operated bank. We could print it ourselves, rather than pay you banksters to give it to us. It's not your money in the first place. It's my money, as President. Maybe we should finally eliminate the middle man, establish a national bank again, and never borrow a dime, nor pay a dime's worth of interest on the money we print, and therefore never go a cent into your debt. How would you like that, Pittance?"

"But then how would you become a billionaire, Hilty? Think about it. Do think it through. What's good for the bankers, is what's good for you. How much money have we bankers paid you for speeches and campaigns and whatnot? Tens of millions? And then you use that money to make even more money, through our banks. Do we not own you, Hilty Crimeton? Did we not make you rich beyond your wildest dreams already?"

"Touché, Viper. But any way you slice it, the government keeps the banks afloat. You banksters couldn't thrive let alone exist without the government."

"Here's another way to look at it, Hilty: if we don't like the government, we won't support it. We'll replace it with a different government. New officials can be selected to run for office, officials who we select, officials who then owe us. So you see, Ms. President, we won't let any government exist that refuses to support us bankers. We bankers need the government business. And you in government need our money to get in power in the first place. Grassroots funded candidates like Alle Peoples are rare. There's only so much money to go around, and we bankers and CEOs own and control most of it. We set the limits, not the government. And as you well know, the top One Percent of the population owns more wealth than the bottom 90 percent. So we can pretty much buy what we want: politicians, Practical Policies, militaries, industries, coin purses, countries, continents, whatever. Business is business. Business rules. We who control the money, control the world."

"It's a coup you banksters pulled years ago. But people are on to you now, Pitt. Justice Assured, Wikilooks, and that whole crowd. Alle Peoples and the rabble. Everyone! They are all out of line, online not least! They know how the game is rigged."

"They think they do, Hilty, but do they really?" said CEO Pittance Viper. "Hell, way back when, auto tycoon Henry Ford said, if people knew how banks and the monetary system really worked, then there would be a revolution by next morning. He thought it was good that people didn't know, and so do I! And President Eisenhower's Treasury Secretary, Anderson, pointed out that 'When a bank makes a loan...the money is not taken from anyone else's deposits; it was not previously paid in to the bank by anyone. It's new money, created by the bank for the use of the borrower.' And that's right! We make up the money: ex nihilo! It's make-believe! But don't you folks at home try it. And don't you officials dare do it in the government. We control the money. We set the limits. Only we wise bankers can be trusted to create money, for anyone we like. Show me the money! Ex nihilo, Baby! Even the Bank of England recently noted that 'The reality of how money is created today differs from the description found in some economics textbooks: Rather than banks receiving deposits when households save and then lending them out, bank lending creates deposits ... whenever a bank makes a loan, it simultaneously creates a matching deposit in the borrower's bank account, thereby creating new money.' Poof: money! Profit first, last, and middle! Total profit! Money is magic. Banker money. But of course I know, like President Crimeton knows, this is the Age of the Internet, and news travels fast! People think they should be allowed to make up their own money. It seems every damn state in the US and far too many cities large and small are pushing to start their own banks. Public banks! To make their own money, fund their own projects. Damn them! We bankers say, No! Over our dead bodies! Over our dead banks! But the internet is making it hard to keep a lid on, Hilty. If only you and I had been born before electricity, before electronics, we wouldn't have to worry about all this BS!"

"I'm telling you, Pitt. Everyone is on to you. Or they will be soon. So you owe me. I can help you, Pitt. I have the Bully Pulpit! So now it's going to cost you a pretty penny, CEO Viper. And you will put that pretty penny direct into my pretty pockets to keep your old-fashioned racket going. I take a hell of a lot of heat for you banksters, more all the time." President Crimeton shook the money purse in CEO Viper's face. "It's going to take mounds more of these smooth beauties to make me a happy, happy President, Pitt. You line up entire train cars, cargo planes, ocean liners full of flesh to keep me focused on the task, CEO Pittance Viper."

CEO Viper squirmed.

Dineh all but threw up.

"It's what you do all the time anyway already, Pitt," said President Crimeton. "With your fees and rates that scalp the people, with the flesh and blood voracious industries and militaries that you fund." Then she turned to Dineh. "This is big, Dineh. Tell him, Viper, tell him about our Practical Policy for making gazillions, and for, you know, solving the Puerto Rican problem."

"As you can see," said CEO Viper, "the President drives a hard bargain. Maybe too hard." He smiled his bony smile.

"Let's get to the policy, Pittance."

"With pleasure. 'A Practical Policy' is the work and genius of my main stat guy and actuarian, Bowns Kruncher. I am happy to take credit for it however."

"You live off credit, Pittance!"

"True, true. The world is one great credit to me!"

"Pittance, you are too modest!

"Facts are facts. And great credit goes to you too, President Crimeton. My clients' superb investment opportunities are made possible by way of your policies. How did that golden boy journalist Gunnar Lapdog once put it?: 'The hidden hand of the market will never work without a hidden fist. McDonald's cannot flourish without McDonnell Douglas, the designer of the US Air Force F-15. And the hidden fist that keeps the world safe for Silicon Valley's technologies to flourish is called the US Army, Air Force, Navy and Marine Corps.... Give war a chance!' That's what he wrote."

"Exactly. Or the banks will never survive!" said President Crimeton.

"Usually, we keep that sort of thing to ourselves. Sometimes Gunnar Lapdog is too reckless in his boasts on behalf of our world. Trying to make himself look good, I suppose, like a man about the globe. Gunnar is a multimillionaire himself. He married well, so we can't knock him too much."

"Pittance, tell Dineh how much money we will make with our new Practical Policy."

"Hundreds of billions. Tens of trillions. Puerto Rico is merely a paradisaical jumping off point. The big money will be pumped in from farther abroad."

"A global harvesting of skin, blood, and bones?" asked Dineh.

"The profits are incalculable!" said President Hilty Crimeton.

"Oh, we can calculate, don't worry," said CEO Viper. "We live or die by very fine calculations indeed. And we don't die. Corporations and banks are eternal. We are no mere mortals. We are immortal. We transcend the physical. And we are everywhere. Banks are gods. And, by extension, bankers."

"You'll make a killing," said Dineh. "You always do."

"I like to look at it as giving birth, to ever

greater banking," said CEO Viper. "We work very hard for our gold. We work like the Devil!"

"The Devil has nothing on you," said Dineh.

"The Devil made me do it!" cackled Hilty Crimeton.

"We are very good at what we do, it's true. Otherwise, we would not do it."

"Okay," said President Crimeton. "Brass tacks, Viper. Nitty Gritty. What is to be done exactly? We need to know in order to best spin it to the public."

"We are going to suck their blood," said CEO Viper.

Dineh felt his ribs pulse. The Money Closet seemed very small.

"Oh, not like that, Dineh," assured President Crimeton. "Not exactly. You can't squeeze a rock for blood."

"The sands, though, sometimes give up liquid gold," said Pittance Viper. "I suppose we won't suck their blood so much as pump it out."

"With big pipes!" said Hilty Crimeton.

"Dineh, you're Puerto Rican, aren't you?" said CEO Viper.

"Navajo."

"Well, that's what I mean. You are not white. Not shiny white like, well, like a lot of us. You are not, you know, pearl white."

"I bleed red, if that's what you mean," said Dineh.

"Not at all. Look, some pearls are brown, I grant you that. Not the most valuable ones, of course. Some are silver. I bought a string once of

30 silver pearls. And some pearls are gold," said CEO Viper.

"I like the gold ones," said Hilty Crimeton. "Unfortunately, most of my pearls are merely white." President Crimeton smiled and fingered those around her neck.

"Your former opponent, Donbo Tyrump, he prefers the white ones. By a lot. The whiter the better."

"My vanquished opponent, you mean," said President Crimeton.

"Are we sure he's really down and out?" said Dineh.

"Gold pearls are the best," continued Hilty Crimeton. "A President should be covered in gold pearls. But that's not what mainly concerns us. Dineh here is not white. And neither are the Puerto Ricans."

"What do you suggest we do with him?" said CEO Viper, a lacerating gleam in his eyes.

"If I'm not mistaken, most people in Puerto Rico consider themselves to be white," said Dineh. "According to the Census Bureau, 75 percent of Puerto Ricans consider themselves so. See, you might want to check with the Puerto Ricans first. I'll tell you right now, my people-"

"Is this a problem?" President Crimeton asked CEO Viper.

"Hardly. After all, the people of the Rich Port don't look white, most of them. That's what really matters. And they are poor. Again, most. Poor white versus rich white - big difference. Anyway, poor brown versus not so poor brown -

not always a huge difference. Marketing and financing won't be a problem. Puerto Ricans, and the like, they owe whatever wealth they might have to their flesh and blood, literally. That's where we bankers come in."

"Puerto Ricans are US citizens, remember," said President Crimeton. "Could be an issue. Flesh-and-blood payments are extracted more easily from non-citizens abroad."

"Or from prisoners here," Dineh noted. "They truly work for slave wages. And the inner cities and abandoned countrysides. Aren't many people there not more or less defenseless now? What do they have to fall back on?"

"Bankers! Us! Dineh? Are you feeling ill again? Please," said CEO Viper. "The majority of Americans don't even know that Puerto Ricans are US citizens, even if Puerto Ricans do. Mainlanders think Puerto Ricans live on Planet Other, when they think of them at all. The schools for the poor - pardon me - the public schools, they don't much address the triflings of who lives where and why and how, let alone who dies where and why and how, let alone who owns who and why and how and where. It hardly matters: the people don't need to know anything. They've got sports and music and video and porn and food and drink and drugs and cars and clothes and this and that and whatever to keep them distracted. That's why the internet is so helpful and so dangerous at the same time. These goddamned outlaw hackers that call themselves scientific journalists, that filching Wikilooks!

They use Instasnapfacetwit to reveal too much! Goddamn that Justice Assured! Can't you drone those outlaws, Hilty?"

"Oh, I've looked into it, Viper. Everyone and their brother in the media and in government and beyond have been calling for his head. Literally."

"Well, I would certainly hope that you've looked into it, Hilty, after all the money we've paid you. And?"

President Crimeton glanced at Dineh. "I shouldn't say, here, in mixed company."

"You're not going to kill him with your own bare hands, are you Hilty?"

President Hilty Crimeton looked as if she had considered it.

"I know some attorneys, and more than a few judges, who could get you time served easily, Hilty. Pardon my humor. We can't be too careful, but thankfully it doesn't matter most of the time who knows what. Everybody knows the dice are loaded. What would people do even if they did know how every little thing that we so readily arrange - fees, debts, rates, laws, guns, rulers, cops, soldiers, surveillance, and money, money, money - puts them in their place and keeps them there? What *could* they do? Common people need to learn to be accepting and to bear up. Just take a look at that outlaw Justice Assured and Wikilooks, and Shallsee Manifest in the hole, and Forward Showem trapped in Russia. Those guys, like Puerto Rico, are in no position to negotiate. And those big mouths came from relative privilege. Think of the poor suckers at the bottom of the heap. What chance do they have?"

"Almost no chance, it looks," said Dineh.

"No. No chance: period." CEO Viper added, "As long as we stay on our game."

"Puerto Rico is our own private paradise," said President Crimeton. "I do love brown skin. They vote for me a lot."

"True that," said CEO Viper. "Bars Bomba Obomba did us right in Puerto Rico. He signed off on the fantastic Promesa bill that set up the Federal Control Board handpicked by the President and Congress to control Puerto Rico's finances and its public policies and to cap, control, cut social services to pay interest on our bank loans. Creating the Federal Control Board was the only way we banks would see a healthy return on our investment. The people of Puerto Rico aren't going to pay back our loans. From their point of view, why would they, how could they, and with what? We need to force them to pay. They have nothing, or so they think. Their economy is gutted, everyone is in debt. They think of themselves as valueless to the greater good. Now we can harvest their blood, flesh, and bones."

"Plight of the world," said Dineh. "You've got them right where you want them."

"We certainly want them in our debt. It would be terrible to be in their debt."

"As if that could happen."

"I know, right? A joke."

"That the people could own their own

island?"

"Not in my lifetime, Dineh. Puerto Rico is our island now, the bankers' island. It's even named for us: the Rich Port. Beautiful shelter in a storm."

"Over half of Puerto Ricans still have significant Taino ancestry, the original Taino inhabitants," said Dineh. "Maybe they think it's their island. I can't imagine why. Nearly half have West African ancestry, from the Africans originally brought over as slaves. Maybe they think they are owed something too."

"Bullshit, Dineh. An even higher percentage have European ancestry. Don't be ridiculous."

"So then it's only Goldun's island? Puerto Goldun?" said Dineh. "And you sit here in this land, Pilgrim Viper, in Amerigoldun, and not in my land of the Diné? And you don't hesitate to tell me who owns what, and who owns who, do you, Mr. Viper?"

President Hilty Crimeton laughed like a weary bartender. "I told you, Viper. My man, Dineh, here, he's funny. In his precious little way."

The CEO of Goldun Sichos investment bank, Pittance Viper, grimaced. "Ancient history, Dineh, ancient history. Something to talk about sometime over a glass of champagne. This is where I tell you how it is going to work: President Obomba's Federal Control Board plan was a good start but merely a beginning. Obomba performed wonderfully for the banks like we knew he would, after we carefully vetted him prior to his initial run for office. That was why he had our full support and funding from long before Day One. He knew well how to control the Puerto Ricans and the rest, in the US and abroad. He knew well how to control the brainwashed liberals and ignorant conservatives both. The guy knows control. Pardon me, Hilty, I mean no disrespect to your not inconsiderable talents. After all, you nearly beat the guy when you had your chance."

"I'm willing to let bygones be bygones. It's one small happy club. You know, Pittance, Bars Bomba Obomba and myself are night and day better than those jokers from the Clown Party. Everyone knows it's true. That's as plain as the gold in your pocket, Viper."

CEO Pittance Viper grimaced again. "As bankers we would prefer those in power to be those whom you refer to as the Clown Party, that is, the Republicans. Unfortunately, their efforts at mental cleansing do not often match those of the Democrats. So we threw our dollars behind President Bars Obomba just as we now need you, Hilty, to advocate for the Practical Policy we discuss here today."

"I'm afraid to ask," said Dineh. "Does this Practical Policy have anything to do with your new coin purse, Ms. President?"

"We are going to need a second Money Closet, Dineh!"

"And a third and a fourth, I assure you," said Pittance Viper.

"First we must explain the new Practical

Policy to the commoner, to Jane and Joe Handheld," said President Crimeton. "I worry that they will not be able to understand the public need for it."

"Explain, publicly relate, propagandize, mentally cleanse, we'll give them the full Ed Bernays PR treatment, father of modern propaganda, public relations...brainwash! I must defer to you, Ms. President. PR is your career, your expertise. You Democrats have become the main PR firm for Wall Street. Not as clumsy as the Republicans, usually."

"Thank you, Pittance," said President Crimeton. "I'm sure you don't intend to give me too much credit! I'm merely a powerful paid actress, at your bankers' electoral service. For the finer arts of mental cleansing, I use speechwriters. That's how we get what passes for popular approval. We need a speechwriter, for our new Practical Policy."

"Not just any speechwriter," said CEO Viper. "You will want the one who wrote a similar policy a few years ago for the Middle East: The Cannibalization of Iraq, or whatever it was called."

"Come on, Pittance. Be politically correct," cautioned President Crimeton. "Our world depends on it. The Cannibalization of Iraq is found nowhere in our politically correct thesaurus."

"You'll have to lend me a copy, Hilty. I seem to have misplaced mine."

"That policy smashed Iraq," said Dineh.

"Only Jonathan Swift could rewrite the thing now. I believe he has passed on."

"We can revive him," said CEO Viper.

"Paging Dr. Frankenstein," said President Hilty Crimeton.

"All things are possible with money, Dineh," said CEO Viper. "That guy, Swift, he had the right mindset but the wrong attitude. We can do better than Swift ten times over."

"Who's the other guy, the consumer cannibal guy?" asked President Crimeton.

"Pierce Gore! Such prose!" said CEO Viper. "Such style! Such voice!"

"Dineh, call him in. Tell him we have a special job that requires his exquisite services."

"Mr. Attack Iraq? He worked for the opposition."

"He can pivot," said CEO Viper. "He won't need to pivot much. I've got him right here." Pittance Viper tapped his smart phone. "Gore? This is Pittance. I need you here now. Oval Office. Yes, Gore, is there another? You're not out of town, Gore. Don't make me geo-track you. No, you're not in Belize, Gore, though you want to be. The NSA knows too, so don't get wise. I can make a quick call if I have to. The chip in your smartphone tracks you, and the national political police will haul you in, rest assured. The FBI, of course. The NPP, right. Sorry, Gore, you can turn off the geo-chip, but we have our ways. Remote activation, that's correct. Bankers these days need to know, Gore. Right. We control the world, yes. That's correct: money talks, shocks, fokkks.

Absolutely. Outstanding, Gore. You're tired? Well, how could you not be? I saw you last night at Blowies with Merry Lane. She's too modest to be hanging around the likes of you, Gore. I'll have a talk with her, when she comes over for dinner next. No, not in my home! Are you crazy?! A real stunner, yes, lovely, very round. Oh, yes. The Oval Office, Gore. Get here as fast as humanly possible. Listen, I'll make it worth 100 grand for you to show up in a timely manner. A business expense, the bank pays, not me. You don't have to take the job, Gore, but you will. We need a Practical Policy for Puerto Rico, also for South America and Africa. Oceania, too. The entire Southern Hemisphere. All Latin America, yes. We're doing the entire world this time, all at once, all the rest of it. Fine-tuning our previous efforts, enhancing, escalating, all-encompassing, yes. *My* geography is off, Gore? Think again. Obviously Puerto Rico and most of Africa sit above the equator but figuratively speaking it's what is called The South: Latin America, Africa, Oceania. Basically anything south of the Rio Grande, south of the USA - Hell! south of New York City and Washington DC. In and around the Mediterranean and points south. And south of mainland Asia. Well, China may be too big for now. All other points south. Some of the whites excepted, naturally, Gore. No, we can't call them whites, of course. It's not in the politically correct thesaurus, or so I'm told. Don't be crude, Gore, One Percent is not a term we use in our tight circle. No, it's not your own teeth that we will pull to make studded bracelets and cat collars. No, we don't need an all-out Practical Policy for most of Australia and New Zealand. Though the Aussies would go for it right away. That's right, very obedient. I know, Gore, we already drew up this kind of plan for Iraq and Greater Oila during the invasion. And we've pushed these policies worldwide ever since, well basically ever since this nation founded itself as an all expanding, ever entitled Empire. We're fine tuning now, Gore, to the Nth degree, squared, cubed. We're cranking it. It's the big blowout. No, no, we are not going to open human restaurants. There's no market share for that - it's inexplicable but the world is tending vegetarian. That's right, Gore, human stock can be used in other products. Of course we initiated global consumption of human bodies long ago. We're cranking it up again. And why not? There are ever more bodies on Earth. So what's past is present anew. What's present is future only moreso. He who controls the past controls the present, he who controls the present controls the future, he who controls the future controls the money, okay, and he who has the money rules! Don't be dense, Gore, we're making it official now. John Jay, first Chief Justice of the US Supreme Court: "Those who own the country ought to govern it." It's as American as apple pie, as American as Empire, yes, as American as, well, European! As American as Manifest Destiny, exactly. But things are threatening to slip. It's this goddamned Internet Age. Transparency and all that bullshit. We've got to thread the screws tighter now while we still can. Crimeton, yes. President Crimeton. Every election is a fresh start for us, Gore, a windfall. People think it's new. A little, at least. Yes, get here fast, my man, before I give this job to any one of the interns who could write it in no time. Every good political science graduate student, that's right. And econ majors. It's a great age to be an econ, Gore, believe me. I know you must. You'll thank me later. You always do. Merry Lane wants to see you many times over, Gore, though I'll warn her about you. Yes, she wants you with your money. Filch you too, Gore, you filching bastard." Pittance ended the call.

"That was so uplifting, Pitt!" said President Crimeton. "Your straight talk, it's so refreshing!"

Dineh clutched his ribs.

"Writers," CEO Pitt Viper muttered. "They're like children who grow up with no parents, no direction. They think they know things. They think it matters. They need to be steered like a damned boat, like a battle cruiser, like a dog on a leash, we need to make sure they point their guns and fangs in the right direction."

"No need to guide Pierce Gore," said President Hilty Crimeton. "He had the right sort of parents."

"I'm sure you are right, Hilty. In fact, I know you are. Pierce Gore has always been on point in the past. And you, Ms. President, have always been so right. Got a lot of Goldwater Girl in you still. I've read how proud you remain about your work for that pale old Republican skinflint back in the day. The things you get away with, Hilty, kissing up to that bloody Kissinger too in public. How many nations did he tear through? You truly are a Wondergirl. No blood on you, Ms. President. Deft, truly deft. Well, you have money on your side. Doesn't hurt."

"We all have a past, Pittance."

"And an even greater future!"

The President and the CEO high-fived.

"Deal me in, Viper," said Hilty Crimeton.

"We already have. Now I'm going to ask you to prove yourself once again. By any chance, might you have cash on hand to make a loaner?" He tapped the money cabinet behind him. "I just promised 100 grand to Gore and I've only got 50 on my person."

President Crimeton grinned. "Happy to lend a hand, Pittance. You know me too well." Dineh tapped a code on a number pad on the wall. Then President Crimeton pulled open a drawer of the money cabinet behind her and lifted out a band of bills. She kissed the money, then handed it over to CEO Pittance Viper. "You know me too well," she said again.

"Keeping tabs on you, that's my job. Thank you." CEO Viper accepted the money from President Crimeton, then reached into a suit pocket and pulled out a band of bills.

Dineh wondered what might be stashed in the other pockets. He imagined bloody things.

"I charge interest at a rate you'll admire, Pittance," said President Crimeton.

"Terrific, Hilty. And well you should."

"Dineh, cancel the rest of my appointments for today. I know I've got half the globe waiting, the Euro U, this Kingdom and that Kingdom... whatever. Today, we are the only Kingdom that matters."

Dineh checked his smartphone. "And representatives from Russia and China too are now requesting a word with you, Ms. President."

"Tell them to get a room. This is a once in an Empire opportunity for me. A dynastic delight, I mean. Sometimes I forget the correct words. Dynasty it is. Very 'nastic! Pittance and I have some details to work out. We need to incorporate some of the other Crimeton family members and the Crimeton Foundation itself into the institutional vortex of the Practical Policy."

Suddenly there was a knock on the door of the Money Closet.

"Vice President Fonie Fleece has arrived for a meeting," said the President's receptionist.

"Tell him to go away, Dineh," said President Crimeton.

"He's the Vice President of the United States of America. Where would he go?"

"China, I don't care," said President Crimeton. "Oh, all right, send him in. He can have your seat. I'm sure speechwriter Gore will be here soon. You can prep him in the Oval Office if you like. Make sure he knows what we want."

"You needn't worry, Ms. President," said CEO Viper. "Pierce Gore is very sharp."

"Dineh, I order you to worry. Quiz him. Make

sure he gets it. I'll holler when we're all set in here."

And with that, Dineh withdrew from the Money Closet, passing Vice President Fonie Fleece in the hall.

III.

Dineh met speechwriter Pierce Gore in the Oval Office where he and Gore seated themselves across from one another on couches flanking a coffee table.

"Where is the fighter-bomber statue?" asked Gore, noting its absence from the President's desk.

"In the money room. You'll see in a minute. The President needs a major policy speech. I'm to review it with you."

"I knew I would get a call when the flesh was about to hit the turbines."

"CEO Pittance Viper and President Crimeton want an updated version of your Attack Iraq speech."

Speechwriter Gore shrugged. "I modified the beginning of it on the way over here. Then expanded from there. A new Practical Policy for the rest of the world, everywhere the US currently owns a military installation. That is, in almost every country, even Cuba, apart from Russia and China."

"Taiwan, though. There too. Remember, Gore, China considers Taiwan to be part of China.

How could it not? Taiwan's official name is the Republic of China! So, US military bases and deployments in China too. Probably even in Russia. Certainly on its immediate borders. In a very real sense the US military occupies every ocean, every continent, and nearly ever country, surrounding the few it may not."

"Guns! God! And Gold!" said Pierce Gore. "What every growing American boy needs. As American as apple pie."

"Apples are from Asia, Gore."

Pierce Gore shrugged. "Seems fitting."

"Here's what they want, Gore," said Dineh. "The new Practical Policy is to begin in Puerto Rico."

"Lovely island, Puerto Rico, the Rich Coast, Port of Paradise."

"Deeply indebted, poverty-stricken."

"Not the parts I visit. Tell me, Dineh, you're Puerto Rican?"

"Navajo."

"That's what I mean. Navajos and Puerto Ricans are both descended from the same people who came across the Bering Strait a long time ago. I know my history, Dineh."

"Are you human, Gore? If so, then you're African. More than 300,000 years ago a certain group of hominids in Africa split three ways, at least. Two of those groups left Africa. One group lived in Europe and Asia and became the Neanderthal species. Another group lived in Asia and Oceania and became the Denisovan species. The group that stayed in Africa became the

Sapiens species from which humans are mainly descended. About 60,000 years ago, the Sapiens species came out of Africa and mated with its long lost relatives the Neanderthals in Europe and Asia and with the Denisovans in Asia and Oceania. Today, no Denisovans and no Neanderthals remain, apart from genetic traces. That's right, Gore, humans came out of Africa and mated marginally with relatives who had formerly come out of Africa, so that today, everyone, meaning all humans, have less than six percent Neanderthal and Denisovan genetic material, and most sub-Saharan Africans have no genetic material from Neanderthals and Denisovans at all, making them the most Sapiens of all! So, when I say that I am Navajo, I am saying that I came out of Africa, originally, as did your people, two times over. Hey, stats, Gore! As a Navajo, I am slightly more Denisovan and Neanderthal than you, and you of European descent are slightly more Denisovan and Neanderthal than Africans, most of whom are not Denisovan or Neanderthal at all. Get it? All people are of 100 percent African descent, 100 percent human, and all with genetic materials entirely or almost entirely from the Sapiens species. Race is bullshit. There is a far greater degree of difference between people within so-called races than across races."

"Do you mean to tell me, Dineh, that Africans are the only pure blood humans?"

"There's one human species, Gore. It has a complex history, beginning in Africa, and sweeping out from there."

"Well, if all that's true, don't tell the Klan they got it backwards all these years, that they are the impure ones! No Neanderthal in African blood and genes. No Denisovan. Only Sapiens!"

"Proud Neanderthals that the Klan are, Gore, I don't think it will bother them much. Sapiens meaning wise, meaning human. The Neanderthals and the Denisovans added some diversity to the gene pool, Gore. That's the irony for the brute crusaders against diversity. But the idea of white supremacy is insane in many ways. And by Klan, Gore, do you mean the neo-KKK elements of the Democratic Party and Republican Party especially? Did you see the report? White supremacy is stronger in the US than in apartheid South Africa."

"But how can it possibly be true that we are all Africans, one species, no races?! Next you'll be telling me that all the Gods of all the religions are totally imaginary, make-believe, made-up!"

"Now that you mention it."

"How can at least one religion not be true?!"

"Which one?"

"Any one?!"

"In truth, no one knows."

"Without God, Dineh, how can we tell people what to believe, what to do and not do, how to act, what to think, what to say, what to write, what to Instasnapfacetwit? How can we keep them from our throats?! How will the people find purpose in life?"

"How to keep the people from your wallet

and banks, Gore? I'll tell you how: equality. Of condition. One of the old Enlightenment ideals. Liberty, equality, solidarity. As for life, it's what you make make it. People give meaning to life. All Gods so far dreamed up are pure and total fictions. As far anyone knows."

"Look, Gods are one thing. But race! I can see race. How can race be a fiction?"

"Race is made up too, Gore. It has meaning today because people give it meaning. The perverse idea of white supremacy forces race into existence. So too are all religions made up, you know, socially constructed. Catholics are made up, Protestants are made up, Muslims are made up, Jews are made up, Christians are made up, Mormons are really made up! Scientologists are made up. Go back through history, myth, religion, literature, and pick your Gods - all made up! Genetics isn't made up, Gore, and if we go by genetics, then people are people, a single species. A species on the brink that badly needs to get its act together."

"But race is, I mean, it has to be, you know, look around you."

"My people came out of Africa, originally, with your people."

"No, I mean-"

"What you mean is that I have brown skin, the color of cooked hamburger, and equally salable, and you don't."

Pierce Gore stared curiously at Dineh. "Are you angling for my job?"

"And now you will update the Attack Iraq

Practical Policy for the world, or you will not leave with your $100,000 advance. I expect that the President and CEO will want an entire book from you this time, to better fashion respectable opinion."

"Where did you say President Crimeton and CEO Viper were meeting? In a money room?"

"It's across the hall."

"Can't wait to see it. So, President Crimeton wants you to hear what I've got first? Time is money, especially her time."

Speechwriter Gore tapped his handheld.

"Tell me how this sounds: 'A Practical Policy: For Saving the People from Themselves, in Puerto Rico, the Global South, and Beyond, and for Making Them Beneficial to the Global Economy'. That covers it, yes?"

"Close enough," said Dineh. "Shoot straight and don't miss. I'm sure you won't." Dineh's ribs throbbed, as speechwriter Pierce Gore began to read through his draft.

IV.
A Practical Policy

For Saving the People from Themselves, in Puerto Rico, the Global South, and Beyond, and for Making Them Beneficial to the Global Economy

"It is a melancholy object to observe the plight of children in the ancient land of

Puerto Rico and the Global South during this era of US dominance. Trapped in disemboweled economies, parents often find themselves unable to provide for their children's basic needs – nutritional, educational, medicinal, limbnal.

"By now, it can only be agreed by all sane observers that the grotesque mortality rate and mass suffering of the children of Puerto Rico and the Global South cannot be considered worth even the most high-minded motives of economic powers; and, therefore whatever might be discovered to be a just, affordable, and compassionate solution to this dreadful situation should be implemented immediately – A Practical Policy.

"It seems only fair that any such policy benefit not only the children of Puerto Rico and the Global South but also those people whose power and authority is needed to enact the solution – the Americans, and other rulers of the world, the global elite, the plutocracy, that is, the great leaders of nation-states, executives of transnational corporations, as well as bankers and privileged investors in whose care rests the prosperity of civilization.

"And so we judiciously advance A Practical Policy, which we expect will not be liable to the least objection, for easing the troubled situation of children around the world.

"It is our well-reasoned advice that there be a globally implemented and internationally regulated expansion of commercial trafficking in children.

"In other words, the time has long since come to officially sanction the body parts trade – and the many corporate byproducts and fiscal derivatives to be reaped thereof. The US government has recently been advised by myriad corporate and financial executives at home and abroad that the children of impoverished nations especially, though not solely, are coming to be understood in more and more explicit terms as the next great global growth industry – children as a prolific cash crop.

"The children would be harvested for their own sake, and be mercifully removed from hopeless predicaments of hunger, disease, danger. In many cases, the children might be sold abroad, their cut-rate labor placed in the service of others in more profitable situations. As well or better, the children could simply be released from their agonizing, degraded state of being – that is, they would be terminated, offered as providence for those fortunate enough to live in more bountiful circumstances.

"Regrettably, in Puerto Rico and the Global South nowadays medicines and food are so expensive, scarce, or non-existent that children might best be sold or traded and shipped out of country at the first onset of illness or hunger, or even at birth, given their likely grim future. Alternatively, for any children who survive well into their youth, these plucky young creatures should be allowed every opportunity to market themselves piecemeal or in whole for distribution and handling abroad. The children are truly our future.

"It only makes smart business sense that the children, along with certain adults – prisoners, the indigent, prostitutes, vagrants, and other wretches – be bought and sold under international regulation, as opposed to the chaotic, unauthorized, and inefficient current illicit manner – perhaps as defined and implemented by a new round of global trade agreements, or by some minor modification of the preeminent institutions for global economic development, the World Trade Organization, the International Monetary Fund, and Wall Street, the US Military, and the US State Department. By auctioning off children, impoverished countries – and, indeed, the poor sectors of rich countries also – may raise much badly needed capital for paying off debts to creditors, US banks especially.

"As one might expect, the nature of the

vending process would be multifaceted. Older children and adults might distribute themselves via body part sales – a kidney here, a lung there. We are informed by numerous industry specialists that discreet patches and strips of tender young skin can be safely peeled off and sold as raw material for the manufacture of leather car seats or even for exceptionally fine wallets and unique handbags, stylish purses, high end couches. Today's global youth should be as thrifty and imaginative with their bodies as possible so that in this way they might pay for water, food, medicine, shelter, and schooling where possible.

"Why not give youth and adult wretches the opportunity to legally pursue a broader, more lucrative array of commercial opportunities, such as the well-regulated sale of their skin, flesh, and non-vital organs? So many older youth are already engaged in the practice of renting their bodies and lives to diverse employers for insufficient wages, where feasible, so why not encourage these young ones to legally take the logical next step of further integrating themselves into the market by scraping off bits of themselves and bargaining with their very blood, flesh, and bones?

"Parents as well might wish to trade abroad any number of infants to help

support the household. The potential
commercial possibilities and personal
recompense for both children and parents
alike seem virtually infinite – nevermind
the boost such inspired activity would
give to any country's Gross Domestic
Product, tying more tightly each national
economy to the dominant forces of the
global market, US banks not least.
Revenue raised by exporting children
from youth-rich regions might also be
spent on quality lifestyle imports such as
cigarettes, coca-cola, and military
armaments that the US produces in huge
abundance, and distributes and advertises
intensely for the betterment of humankind
everywhere. In this manner, rich sectors
might profitably advance more effectively
a sort of compassionate-cannibalism for
the improvement of youth and their
superiors the world over.

"There may be some naysayers who
doubt the possible financial benefits of a
globally regulated traffic in children and
other wretches, either piecemeal or in
whole. These skeptics would do well to
consider the sound advice and impressive
data gathered from a wide variety of
world-renowned investment bankers,
politicians, chief executing officers, media
magnates, military commanders, cooks,
upholsters, fashion experts, and many
others. This data indicates that simply by

harvesting the non-vital organs of several moderately healthy young children, a family of four may provide themselves with their minimal nutritional requirements for several months, under favorable market conditions. Currently, such estimable enterprise would involve selling off youth organs in non-food related ventures, rather than consuming young flesh directly or marketing it to local grocery stores. Times being as lean as they are for the world's majority – direct consumption of youth victuals is not as economically feasible as it was centuries ago during the age of that master humanitarian policy planner, Jonathan Swift.

"This Practical Policy, which the United States intends in all modesty, might at first sound too optimistic in aim and content. Some of the brightest students of world affairs may wonder if there is some prohibitive limiting factor overlooked. On the contrary. Much of what recently seemed unthinkable throughout the world, due to stubborn lack of popular appeal among people everywhere, now has become far more highly regarded by the corporate elite that takes care of us all. Though in the past a boy or girl or any minor or other wretch was no easily salable commodity, the modern reality is that largely due to IMF and World Bank-imposed structural adjustments, and due to ever more vigorous US economic and military activity and control, the global market is now far more wide open than ever to the commerce of flesh and blood and bone..."

"Okay, enough!" said Dineh. "You nailed it, Gore. You hit it right on the head. Congratulations, that's a real piece of work. The Attack Iraq Practical Policy hardly needed to be modified at all. Now along with Iraq, Afghanistan, Syria, and Libya, et cetera, et cetera, et cetera, Puerto Rico and much of the Global South are bankrupt. Hell, even southern Europe, Greece, has been smashed. Economies are gutted. Unemployment astronomical. State of the world."

"Go ahead, try to angle for my lucrative job, Dineh, you won't get it!" said speechwriter Pierce Gore. "To be a great writer, Dineh, you need to know how to polish the wisdom of the corporate elite, the One Percent, those who own the publishing houses, printing presses, giant media and internet companies. You have to give them what they want to hear and what they find useful to know. You have to show them that you can write in ways that keep people from getting too restless, too outraged, too curious. You don't want your readers to be knowing too many things, Dineh. Rather, you want them to think that they know things. It has been said that use of plenty of key facts and realities of life is at the core of great writing, but far more important is pushing great attitude in literature! It's attitude, the proper attitude that matters most in writing as in life. Not the facts, for God's sake! Attitude: 'Look on the sunny side while standing in the muck,' and all that nonsense. I don't believe a word of it myself, Dineh, but I know how to write it, and I know why I must."

"All in for Empire," said Dineh.

"Empire all in!" said Pierce Gore. "You got it, Dineh. Of course, you'll never see me sell myself at a flesh station. You have to know where to sell yourself, Dineh: where it really pays. No, I won't part with so much as the dead tip of a fingernail, personally. But I can fully understand why poor kids, hell, working class kids and adults would feel the need to sell off their blood, organs, and bones. Even their very lives, Dineh! It makes me feel good that I can help them feel proud, even nationalistic, about doing so. You see, Dineh, for great writing in general, you want to cultivate a self-admiring and accepting readership. You need to show the powerful corporate, government, and academic publishing higher-ups that you know how to convince people to go along with what is best for them and for the country that they owe. You need to show people how to be worthy of the grand designs of Empire in what is called modern democracy. You need an infinite knowledge of popular diversions to tempt and tease people into a beautiful alignment. What makes contemporary civilization work so well, Dineh, is a kind of unthinking acceptance of the One Percent way. This is the best kind of obedience, Dineh, when the people don't know the real role they play even as they think they do, the duped liberals, the blinded conservatives. CEO Viper taught me that. We're talking about the honest ones, Dineh, let alone the liars. They are such pawns. I don't mean to belittle that type of mindset, Dineh. They should be happy to be pawns in a great kingdom that covers the globe. And I try to help make them happy. That's where I found my voice."

"You sound as if you have no choice," said Dineh. "You sound as if there is no choice."

"I go where the opportunity is," said Pierce Gore. "I know my position. I know all our position. What could the people do if they did know how owned they are, from top to bottom, from politics to economics, from land to air, water to space, from finance to romance, from control to patrol, from surveillance to ignorance? Who are they to stop it, change it? Who are they to protest much at all? They kind of know, don't they? They get a lot of details wrong and turn on each other, aim at the wrong things, but they kind of know how owned they are."

"It's hard to make change," said Dineh. "But that doesn't mean you go around knifing people with words. It should mean the opposite. Instead, the name of socialism has been smeared as evil. Peace is associated with idiocy. Equality with tyranny. Liberty with military. And unity impossible. Minds cleansed, brains washed, mental traps set, no way out."

"Precisely, Dineh. There is no point in resistance, which is counter-productive to going along to get along. Look at how well I've done! Everything is worked out for people. The One Percent way is life as we know it, the good life of our nation, the affluent life in the towns, cities, countryside, the good life of the planet, as the corporate rulers see fit and know best."

"Except it isn't," said Dineh. "A lot of people live in shit. Or die in it. Or suffer through, hardly able to tell if and how they're living or dying."

"This is the world that we know, Dineh. Writing is profitable, for the right sort. Talented, respectable writers such as myself, the last thing we want to do is to stir up opposition, discord, and counter ideas in our work, Dineh. That would be ideological, clunky, and low art, or no art at all."

"Your words are phony, Gore. And you're killing people with what you write."

"I'm a great writer. I found my voice. You may despise what I write, your opinion, but you must admire what I do. I can really write, Dineh, and I know it. Great writing is a delicate and fine art most pleasing to the One Percent, to be petted and toasted, to be passed around for relaxation, maybe to be lovingly chided at times, but always to be used for adornment. It's not partisan! Facts are a kind of butchery that need to be cosmetically concealed! Great writing purifies the mind! Great writing is a great cleansing! Great writing makes everyone think better of themselves or simply allows for blowing off steam. These are the great uses of great writing. Of course great writing molds minds but we don't speak of this publicly, Dineh, because I'm telling you that the best writers never want to give too many people too many ideas about, well, getting many ideas. That would not be harmonious, now would it, Dineh?"

"You certainly write like the Devil, Gore. Your writing serves you well."

"Thank you, Dineh. Everyone agrees. It doesn't hurt that my family goes way back with the rulers of this land, farther back than you can imagine."

"Pre-Columbus?" said Dineh.

"Well ... far enough," said Pierce Gore. "Besides, I am the best with words and always have been. You are too simple, Dineh. You lack both the purity and the precision of speech that comes with studied nuance, and subtlety, limning to the right word, in the right way."

"There must be something genetically wrong with me," said Dineh.

"I'm sure you can't help it, Dineh. Because if you could, no one around here would tolerate your odd verbal tics for an Einsteinian instant. There's this lunatic, John Doe Dimslow of Appalachia, Dineh, a frightening figure, who wrote a book called "Fiction Gutted," in which he butchers everything wise and good. I stopped reading almost at the start. It goes to show the extreme bounds of insanity in this world, Dineh. This unhinged sort of thing is what is to be feared going viral in lit circles but so far it has stayed deep underground, where it belongs. But John Doe Dimslow reminds me of you sometimes, Dineh. You are too ideological with some of your odd ramblings. Too loaded, too freighted, too biased. You are too repetitious, Dineh. You come across too strong. Your words are impure, unlike mine. I can't wait to hear what President Hilty Crimeton and Goldun Sichos CEO Pittance Viper have to say about my renewed Practical Policy today, Dineh. The language, it's all in the language. You have to know how to spin it. Content comes and content goes, but spin lasts forever. Language is. No one remembers who was starving whom in Jonathan Swift's ancient 'Practical Policy,' what did he call it? 'A Modest Proposal'? Who was starving whom? Who knows?!"

"The rich were starving the poor."

"Whatever."

"They still are."

"It might as well have been Martians and Neptunians for all anyone cares or can recall. No, what we remember is the spin of the tale. How gleefully smug, playfully sober, how ripping good fun it all was. Fine gloves and dress boots fashioned from the flayed carcass of a working class child! What creativity! What language! This is the kind of thing to which I aspire day and night, Dineh. In a few years, no one will remember who exactly was priming the flesh stations with whom, but our modern Empire will be stronger than ever and I will be more well known and more well off. And that's how you do it. Granted, my line of work is not for the weak, Dineh. Nor for the untalented. I warn you, do not try to follow where you dare not tread."

"You are so right, Pierce. You are right to the core. You are so far beyond genius, so high above all that I will never be able to think, let alone write, like you. Congratulations, Pierce. You win."

"Thank you, again, Dineh. Even if you don't mean it, I do. Winning is my specialty. I run, ride, and write with the winners, Dineh, and I always will."

V.

Suddenly Dineh and Pierce Gore heard screams and strange shouts and general chaos.

It sounded like someone was being killed. Or killing. Or both.

Dineh and Pierce Gore ran into the hall, where Dineh saw the National Security Agency Director Allsee Allhear Allspy sitting in front of Dineh's own workstation tapping furiously on the numerical keypad. He was yelling mutant obscenities.

"What happened? What's going on?" asked Pierce Gore. Smoke and the stench of burned flesh pulsed from beneath the locked Money Closet door.

"They locked themselves in! They needed me to get them out!" said Director Allspy. "I had the code. I thought I had the code..."

Baffled, Dineh tried to comprehend. The Director must be lying, but why?

President Crimeton would contact only Dineh for any difficulties.

Whatever the case, Director Allspy must have failed to decipher that the security code for the Money Closet was biometrically programmed to work only within proximity to large amounts of Dineh's DNA. Any other attempt to use the code would be considered a hostile entry attempt, automatically triggering the protective walls of lasers in the Money Closet.

"Give me that!" shouted Dineh. He grabbed the keyboard from the trembling hands of the NSA Director, and quickly remotely deactivated the lasers and unlocked the door.

"What are you doing here?!" Dineh shouted at the Director.

The director seemed in shock. "They locked themselves in! They called me to open the door! I don't know what went wrong!"

"You liar!" screamed Dineh. "What did you want, the gold?!"

"The Gold! The Gold!" said Director Allspy. "Wait - what Gold?"

"It's what you people live for, and so rarely die for!"

Dineh threw open the Money Closet door and was staggered by the smoke and the burnt stench.

Fire alarms blared. Sprinklers poured down water.

Peering inside the Money Closet, Dineh saw the bit of burned rag that had once been President Hilty Crimeton. She had been sitting in the direct line of a wall of lasers. The Vice President had been sitting in Dineh's former seat in another direct line of lasers. He too had been reduced to smoldering rags. The money was unscathed. The lasers were not aimed at the cabinets.

Though shocked by the horrific scene, Dineh realized what had transpired politically. A coup.

Next in line of Presidential succession was the Speaker of the House of Representatives, a member of the opposition party.

Dineh turned and looked back at his computer station. NSA Director Allspy was gone.

"Help me." Goldun Sichos CEO Pittance Viper stood up from his bench. Like the money, he had been untouched by the weaponry. Pressed tight against a money cabinet, his bench seat was safely inside the deadly wall of lasers. "I can't get by without going through all this blood," he said.

Did Dineh imagine it, or did he see CEO Viper smile his bony somehow toothless smile?

Dineh felt as if a grenade had exploded in his ribs where Hilty Crimeton had kicked him earlier. Dineh slammed the Money Closet door in CEO Viper's face, and staggered back toward his workstation.

CHAPTER THREE

Interviewer: What do you make of the alleged Russian interference in the recent US Presidential election?

Professor Knowem Clearsky: My guess is that most of the world is just collapsing in laughter. Suppose all the charges are true, I mean every single one, it is so amateurish by US standards that you can hardly even laugh. Look at what the US does, in country after country, not merely hacking or spreading rumors in the media; but saying look, we're going to starve you to death or kill you or destroy you unless you vote the way we want. I mean that's what we do. Take the famous 9/11, let's think about it for a minute. It was a pretty awful terrorist act. It could have been a lot worse. Now let's suppose that instead of the plane being downed in Pennsylvania by passengers, suppose it had hit its target, which was probably the White House. Now suppose it had killed the president. Suppose that plans had been set for a military coup to take over the government. And right away, immediately 50,000 people were killed, 700,000 tortured. A bunch of economists were brought in from Afghanistan, let's call them the "Kandahar Boys," who very quickly destroyed the economy, and established a dictatorship which devastated the country. That would have been a lot worse than 9/11. It happened: the first 9/11, it happened on September 11, 1973, in Chile. We did it. Was that interfering or hacking a party? This record is all over the world, constantly overthrowing governments, invading, forcing people to follow what we call democracy, as in the cases I mentioned. As I say, if every charge is accurate, it's a joke, and I'm sure half the world is collapsing in laughter about this, because people outside the United States know it. You don't have to tell people in Chile about the first 9/11.

Death by Neptune

"*D*ineh! Wake up! What?! Are you daydreaming? Wake up, Dineh!"

Presidential aide Dineh turned his gaze from the beautiful greenery outside the Oval Office windows. He stood to the left of President Tyrump behind the Oval Office desk.

"Mr. President, ever since the election, it has been so crazy. It's hard to know where we are sometimes."

President Donbo King Tyrump sat at the Oval Office desk with a small spray bottle in his hands.

"Don't be a moron, Dineh. You are right here with me. We have a country at our disposal, a world at our whim. We won."

"Who can believe it? Can you believe it? Maybe we are all dreaming."

"Don't you believe it, Dineh. We won even though we lost! To hell with the popular vote! What is this, a democracy? Don't be an idiot! We won even though everyone said we would not. Losers. Well, guess what, Dineh? The Losers lost!

Time to build a wall, Dineh, a wall that will dwarf the Great Wall of China, those Losers! Time to make this country great again, with our own great wall! We want only the right people in our land, Dineh, the right people who will work hard for the gold that will make this country great again. No Losers Allowed! NLA! Right?! Nobody thought I would win, Dineh. Nobody. But we had some good computer guys. Guys who really know a thing or two about computers. And how they work."

US President Donbo King Tyrump sat at his desk in the Oval Office with a little bottle of specially formulated nasal spray. He squeezed the bottle to shoot the potent liquid up each nostril. Then he threw his head back, and shook it. He breathed deep. He handed the spray bottle to Dineh who slipped it into a pocket for later recycling. President Donbo King Tyrump kept a carton of these precious little bottles in a locked special compartment newly affixed to the walnut wood of the presidential desk.

"You proved them all wrong, Sir," said Dineh. "The election, it was yours for the taking. They should have seen it coming. We all should have seen it coming, Mr. President. It's like nothing we have ever seen before. But that doesn't mean we couldn't see it coming at a million miles per hour."

"I knew I would win, Dineh. The FBI was on my side. Plus, Hilty Crimeton is colossally incompetent. Pitiful. I'm not even exaggerating this time. She had no rural outreach program! In dairy country! What the hell?! Did she think the cows loved her? Honestly, I think she did! She doesn't even know where she is living. She doesn't know what time it is. I can sit in Tyrump Tower my whole life and still know more than that. You've got to appeal to the cows, Dineh, the whole herd. You've got to give the herd a reason to follow you. A Big League reason. You've got to aspire to greatness! Throw some cabbage around, or whatever it is that cows eat before they become red meat. You've got to build walls. And bricks. And roads. You've got to dig coal. You've got to put down the little guys you don't like! Pick on the Losers with low energy! You've got to promise jobs, jobs, and more jobs! Jobs that will fall from the sky! You've got to praise the good people of the world, especially the white people without exactly saying so, because guess what, Dineh? There are still more white people than anyone else around here. Besides, just between you and me, white makes right, who says it doesn't? Even former President Bars Bomba Obomba had rural outreach operations during his campaigns. President Bars! Hilty Crimeton had no economic change program at a time when people wanted one thing and one thing only. Change! I mean, I don't know why she got a single vote! I'm such a likable fellow! She ran on more of the Bars Obomba same! Who does that?! Thank you, Hilty Crimeton! So what that we lost the popular vote by millions?! This is America, we don't need too much democracy here. We are a Republic. A state of states! Estates and more estates! The Incorporated Estates of America!"

"Land that we love," said Dineh.

"Land that we own, Dineh!"

"This land is my land, this land is your land," said Dineh.

"This land is Bank of America's land! This land is my land! Tyrumpland! That's why I'm President and you're not, Dineh."

"Plus, you're a billionaire."

"I hit the right notes. Right on the button! I don't believe a word about the voting machines being tweaked in key states, do you, Dineh? Of course not. I don't care what anyone says. Twenty states? Three states? It can't be true. The machines obviously weren't tweaked well enough to win the popular vote, now were they? We didn't need any tweaks after all. The Electoral College is such a wonderful thing: the right person can win, even when he loses! Time and again! You don't want too much democracy, Dineh. You want the Electoral College, working as designed! Let's say we did tweak the machines, which we didn't - I'm certain - who could tell? There's no paper trail on some of them, no electronic trail on others, no trail at all. Oh well, maybe that's a problem we'll take advantage, I mean, care of next time. Nevermind that these electronic voting machines were designed and maintained by my natural allies: corporate America. Sure, certain people stand to benefit Big League with me in power. Better me than Hilty Crimeton! The people love me! Some of them. The rest can grin and bear it. Filch 'em, Dineh, if they can't take a joke! They got to win the popular vote. I got to win the Presidency. That seems fair. Maybe some tweaks will be needed in the future. Who can tell? We're the winners, Dineh. We won. The Losers, they lost. The world is now set perfectly right. The future never looked brighter."

"What's past is past," said Dineh.

"Outstanding, Dineh. And what lies ahead is the future. And he who controls the future..."

"Makes big bank?"

"The biggest!"

"Mr. President, speaking of the future, a lot of people say that the Sword of Damocles overhanging everything is how on Earth does climate change get adequately addressed, before we all get fried, drowned, frozen, famined, and any number of other horrible things?"

"Oh, to Hell with that, Dineh. I've got climate control in Tyrump Tower. That's all I need."

"But the people, Sir. It's as if the rest of the world depends on the Native Americans like those in pitched battle with US police over fossil fuel pipelines in the Dakotas. Where I grew up in the 'Indian Center of the US' in Gallup, New Mexico, the Native American news pages had the most readable and meaningful news stories from across the US and world that I've ever read in any newspaper. So much fluff and stuff otherwise. It doesn't look good for the world, I have to say, Mr. President. It looks like the fate of the world was decided in the Democratic primary, when Alle Peoples lost. No offense, Sir."

"Don't worry, Dineh. You cannot offend me. I don't regard anyone that highly."

"Thank you, Sir. What I'm saying is that Earth looks to be more of an underdog now than ever. The planet, the climate. And what if someone hacks into the nuclear triad and blows up the world even before we fry or drown or freeze or..."

"You have too much imagination, Dineh. Seriously, you should be a cartoonist. All this is not my concern. I am the winner. I need only think up winning ideas. I need only look after my own interests. And those of my One Percent allies. Sure, I had to appoint people to positions of national and global power. You know who and what they are, Dineh. The Military, Wall Street, the National Security Agencies have been appointed, long since. The corporate elite. Guns, dollars, and spies. The corporate elite and military do it all. That's who I appointed, the guardians of us all here in the One Percent. The corporate executing officers, the banker rulers of the world. They are America's only hope to be great. A mere fraction of a percent, true, but a very important fraction."

"Many people see the One Percent as a mix of opponents and enemies to be defeated, if not won over."

"Many people do not count, Dineh. Ask Hilty Crimeton. Ask Alle Peoples. Don't ask me. I won. You win, you count. You lose, you're a Loser."

"But, Sir, it could all catch up to you rulers, to

power, to you owners, to money, in politics, in everything. The people say that the Republican Party is insane, and that the Democrats are like the walking zombie dead. Meanwhile, Alle Peoples proved he is neither. And even though he lost..."

"The establishment knifed him good, Dineh. It was a real hit and run. You know how it works. What works is what matters. Here you are working."

"Have I ever told you how I got this job, Mr. President? It's a story you would not believe."

"Sure, sure, Dineh. You can tell me some evening at bedtime - that would be, at other people's bedtime. You know how I love to stay up late with my little bottles."

"It seemed like change was going to come, and maybe it has," said Dineh. "Now the old political families are gone, the Bashes and the Crimetons. They appeared strong for years but ultimately no figureheads can last. Were they strong? Or was the public disorganized? I think so. It still is. But Alle Peoples barely organized the public under a New Deal umbrella and almost won it all. And he did it in mere months. You'll need to watch out, Sir. You might need to cut some deals with Alle Peoples."

"He doesn't learn, does he, Dineh? Peoples. He's unteachable. Alle Peoples, or someone like him, will be my number one political problem going forward. I will try to keep Alle Peoples closer than I keep my friends. Legislation, sure. Throw a few bones to the globs of people who want something, the masses, as they're called, why not? We've got lots of bones. Let them gnaw on bones we've already picked clean. Let the people rebuild a few worn down roads and bridges. That'll keep 'em busy. As for Alle Peoples, I'll passive aggressively gut the old bastard. Take any credit that might accrue to him for myself. Or, I'll just slam him down. Whatever works. Make an example of him, again and again. In the meantime, Dineh, you know almost as well as I do who and what remains strong: Wall Street, the military, and the security state, the deep state, working in triangulation together. They have huge budgets, huge economies. Naturally I bowed to the military early on, and of course cozied secretly with Wall Street all along. Otherwise, I owe no one really, a few businesses, not people, though it is useful to owe a few people because then they owe you! They depend on you, for your owing them! But mainly I *own* people. I own! I own! It's off to work I go! No time to say hello, goodbye, I own ... I own, I own, I own. I don't owe, Dineh. I own. I own systems. I own stuff. I own my various brands. I own an email list of millions of people worth tens or hundreds of millions of dollars. I own credit card lists. All built during this election. Hell, you could say I even own the government and the military. I certainly own the Republican Party because the Republican Party was rescued from near certain defeat again, if not for me, Donbo King Tyrump. They owe me, they all owe me. I don't owe anyone, not really. It's not my style."

"They owe who owns them," said Dineh.

"Who said that? Bill Gates? Warren Buffet? Some Saudi King? George Washington? Abraham Lincoln?"

"No, just me," said Dineh.

"Very nice, Dineh, I like it. Well, it takes working together too. The Republican Party and me and Wall Street and the military, we are basically colluding - that's how it works - to increase our wealth and power. None of us sees the game as us versus them. We see it as us together to advance our Top Percent, corporate cream, banker interests.

"It's all good then?" said Dineh.

"Like you can't believe. Lot of good people here. Take my Vice President for example, Rob Loot Thief. Great guy. His best attribute is that he is a dedicated shit-eater and superb liar by profession and temperament. He is highly valued in establishment circles because he is so obedient. He will eat all the shit that I might wish to serve to him, just as I ate my father's shit for so long. This is an important sign of obedience, Dineh. The more shit you eat, the more obedient. And then when you obtain power, you make others eat shit. My Vice President Rob Loot Thief may be genetically programmed to like to eat shit, by all appearances. And he certainly serves up plenty of shit for others to eat."

"It's a wonderful system," said Dineh.

"Well, it is what it is. There's no mystery in this. How it shakes out with my new Presidency is not clear but never can be at first. I've got right

wingers from the Republican Party staffing the
government and setting policy, except modified
by me and my more cosmopolitan family. Plenty
of my business interests are involved, and that of
my family, my son-in-law especially, a real estate
and media powerhouse. Plus, his younger
brother owns insurance companies that have
been making a killing off of Obombacare, so most
of that is safe, unless he moves his money, even
though I've threatened to destroy it. Will people
clap or cry? Who cares, I'm in power now, I'm in
charge. I did what I had to do to win. Then you've
got the military that demands money be
funneled to it, also Wall Street. Some countries
will be destroyed, some won't. Some bones will
be thrown domestically, some won't. People of
color should duck and cover. And you, Dineh, you
should stick close to me. You keep me real,
Dineh. You let me know there are not only rich
white people in the world. You let me know on a
daily basis that other people exist."

"I do what I can, Sir, to not be a Loser."

"You're no Loser, Dineh, or you wouldn't be
anywhere near me. I have to say though, Dineh, it
has been hard lately. I've been having a difficult
time, as you've probably noticed. Being President
of the USA never used to be this way. Look at
what we've come to. Now we are in constant
battle with that verbal terrorist Justice Assured
of Wikilooks, always spilling the beans."

"I believe he refers to himself as a scientific
journalist," said Dineh.

"He's delusional, clearly. He went after Hilty

Crimeton during the election, and we know how pure she is, pure as the wind-driven snow. You don't have to be a scientific journalist to know what colossal bullshit that is. Then I win, he thought she would win, but I win, so now he comes after me. I don't know what it all matters, Dineh. I don't know what it means. I don't really care. I do know that I cannot have somebody breathing down my neck all the time! The situation is intolerable! Totally out of line! It must not stand! If we can't ignore him, we must seek him out, Dineh. We must track him down!"

"He's in London, sitting in his office, imprisoned by the London police in the Ecuadorian embassy. The Ecuadorians continue to protect him," noted Dineh. "The Ecuadorians think they are more civilized than the executing officers of the Incorporated Estates of America. Imagine that. Justice Assured is working at his computer. Probably monitoring us as we speak. You know where he is, Mr. President."

"If only he were American, we could try him for treason and hang him. If we could get our hands on him," said President Tyrump.

"He's Australian."

"Goddamn kangaroos! Why could he not have some other hobby?" said President Tyrump.

"He seems to like this one," said Dineh.

"God damn Justice Assured!" shouted President Tyrump.

II.

The Chief Executing Officer of the World, President Donbo King Tyrump was having a bad day. He had been having a bad month, a bad era even, despite so recently winning the Presidency. So many people seemed to hate him now, with thousands protesting in the streets of cities throughout the country calling *him* the hater! He did not understand why. He had held power in the Oval Office for merely a few months. Well, maybe a little he understood. Okay, maybe a lot. He totally got it. He did it on purpose, made people hate him, the better to win over the bigoted, racist, entitled, ignorant, and otherwise pathological and sociopath vote. Hey, whatever worked. Power demands power. Collateral damage be damned. Why not? After all, candidate Crimeton tried something similar, on a lesser scale. Alle Peoples, that was a different story. Tyrump vowed to crush Alle Peoples when he got the chance. And so it was that being the righteous King of the World came with a bit of a burden: the enmity of the populace. A small weight to bear, which President Donbo King Tyrump, like the Kings of old, was willing to shoulder, for it was nothing in comparison to the perks of power. One thing was certain: the CEO of the World, President Donbo King Tyrump, secretly and not so secretly, happily and not so happily, hated the haters back.

But now things were totally ridiculous. The

once exciting and powerful social and political bubble within which President Tyrump had been free to move had grown smaller by the hour. It was scarcely safe for President Tyrump to relieve his bladder and bowels without a security guard accompanying him to the lip of the toilet. What dignity was there in the CEO of the World shitting in the presence of company?

President Tyrump could no longer sit on his own private toilet and shit in peace without some wiseacre, some subversive, some goddamned invisible, untraceable, unhackable *Socialist* live-streaming the audio to the entire globe. It was probably the work of Justice Assured and Wikilooks. Or Forward Showem, that damned NSA leaker, cooped up in Russia with his dauntless shirtless girlfriend. Or, Hell, it could even be the imprisoned Army whistleblower Shallsee Manifest, somehow outwitting her guards from solitary confinement!

Goddamn it all! Could be Jane and Joe Schmo from Buffalo for all it mattered to the dignity of President Donbo King Tyrump. The very stability of the Kingdom was threatened. The Kingdom – that global alignment of Bankers, Bosses, and Big Business – the One Percent – with the mighty military and spy systems, this was what the CEO President King of the World must protect and preserve at all cost. Otherwise, for whom would he rule? The people? Filch the people. The people did not care about the President's Right Domain. The People cared solely about themselves. Selfish bastards.

The situation was intolerable, absolutely indecent: as soon as the CEO of the World, President Donbo King Tyrump, sat down to shit on his own toilet, or on any other toilet anywhere in the goddamned world, he heard the unsanitary symphony of his royal flatulence decorating the World Wide Web, playing audibly on his daughter's handheld device down the hall, with running commentary and analysis by the goddamned Socialists!

Socialists commenting on the President's shit!

In what righteous regime was the President King CEO of the World forced to listen to the analysis of his own shit?! For the love of the almighty dollar, President Donbo King Tyrump could not parse what was worse, the analysis of his own shit or knowing that his daughter was listening to all that shit!

Other people shit too, by God, they should have to listen to their own shit for a change!

Something had to be done now, damn it! And shit!

President Tyrump was pissed.

He preferred to think of himself as King rather than as President. The King of the World. King Tyrump. The boss. The master of all. King, King, King.

The King tried not to swear in public much. Too many cameras, too many microphones, too many handhelds. All the world was broadcast live all the time anymore. President Tyrump tried not to swear even in private, because what was private? Where was private? Saying shit was more than the nation, any proper nation, could bear. Saying shit in private, truly in private, seemed to the King not only nearly impossible now but less and less effective, even if he often could not help himself. Who cared that this was a shitty world? No need to add shit upon shit these days when he, the King, was in power and in control. Tell that to the goddamned Socialists! Broadcasting his shit everywhere! Did they really think that their own shit did not stink? Filch them.

Filch. There was another word you could not say in public, not a King nor anyone else. No filch in public. The nation could not bear it. What proper nation could? Sure you heard the word almost anywhere and everywhere but not in official rhetoric. Filch, filch, filch. No filch for the King! What was the point? How unKingly to curse like a commoner, like a modern serf, like a gun-toting, computer-packing, debt-lugging vassal. Like a piss-poor voter. CEO President King Donbo Tyrump had standards, now, he sure did, he had bigger things to say. But his own shit was getting smeared all over everywhere, the world, the universe, the beyond if there was a beyond...by the goddamned Socialists!

The royal piss of the thing was that no one knew how the Resistance did it. How on Dearth had the Socialist Resistance invaded the White Palace of the King? The King liked to think of the White House as the White Palace. If only it truly were more grand, less colonial. President Donbo

King Tyrump thought about building another Tyrump tower behind the White House. Something tastefully opulent. Something that his first-class wife Myownia would feel comfortable moving in to. Something glamorous and glitzy. "House" was so mundane, White or not. Common houses were for common debtors.

The King had tried every way possible to keep his shit private. He wore earplugs and cranked rock music. No luck. The Resistance filtered out the sonic blare and broadcast the naked flatulence of the President with the usual Socialist commentary and analysis. This forced President Tyrump to get rid of the music to better hear his own shit, to temper its entrance onto the global scene. Shitting in public was a shitty job.

The White House latrine eavesdropping of the Resistance caused CEO President Donbo King Tyrump to more closely watch his diet. No beans. No eating late in the evening. A Kingdom deserved nights free of the King's daily shit. The King exercised frequently to help control his shit, to make it regular, firm, targeted. Much fiber consumed. The Kingdom deserved no less than perfect shit from the King, if shit it would be made to have.

The King began to shit twice a day exactly, once at dawn while most of the Kingdom slumbered and once before dark after evening meals had passed into the majority of the Kingdom's digestive tracts.

Alas, soon it happened, most people in the

Kingdom no longer set their morning alarms because the King's dawn shit was so loud and public it woke the workers every day. The people rose muttering, "Same shit, same King. Same Kingdom, same shit." A lot of people would add the word, "Filch." Then they would shower to wash the shit out of their ears. Others would turn to their partner and embrace in the most intimate ways. Then they would shower to wash the filch off, before heading out into the shit.

Such was life on planet Dearth deep in the unforgiving Era of Climate Collapse, as the hands of the Doomsday Clock ticked toward midnight. Dearth's Climate was not the only thing far along in the process of change. Or so the Kingdom feared.

How did the Resistance capture the CEO President King's daily shit? When had the spy technology of the Resistance surpassed that of the Spy State itself? How could the Socialists not be destroyed? Perhaps the greater miracle was that the Resistance had not yet captured high definition video to go along with the high fidelity audio of the King's daily shit. CEO President Donbo King Tyrump trembled, waiting for the next layer of shit to drop.

"Only the shittiest of knowledge can save us!" the Socialists declared. "Know your shit!" the Resistance liked to say.

They were derided as shit-rakers. The Resistance embraced the term: Shit rakers arise!

Justice Assured of Wikilooks stated: "The greater the power, the more the need for transparency." "If reporting on power is any good, it is controversial." "Knowledge has always flowed upwards to Kings, not downwards to serfs and slaves."

But now maybe the tide had turned.

"Bring me Justice Assured!" cried Donbo King Tyrump, from his toilet seat.

Dineh thought that future generations, should the human species survive, might be offended by the shitty audio and the crappy use of the word "shit" but not this generation. The King and the Kingdom had seen to that. People today were grateful for the reality made clear amid the official lies, distortions, unimaginable obscenities, and endless garbage emissions from the Korporate Kapital Kingdom that ruled them, beneath which they and the world were sometimes tolerated to survive and work, and often were condemned to suffer and die.

"Shit is the finest word in the English language," declared Victor Hugo in 1862, to freely paraphrase the cultural giant. He dubbed shit "the misérable of words." Victor Hugo was the outraged author of possibly the greatest novel ever written, Les Misérables. The English translator of Hugo's massive three book novel refused to translate that single lowly word shit - "merde" - from French to English because deemed too offensive. Hugo was outraged. In shit in Les Misérables was found life, refuge, victory. And the most shit-splattered people rose to the heights.

So, filch. Every Age suffers from its own

censors, despots, ideological bullshit. And every Age forms its own Resistance. The horrific difference was that this Age was the first Age that might be the Terminal Age of human civilization or even of the human species. It might be the end of human history. Climate change. Nuclear weaponry. Viral attacks. Financial Obliteration. Nuclear weaponry. Climate change. Repeat. There was no time to spare. Filch that shit. Fok it. Hit that shit. The unconscionable heights must be brought justly low. And the Socialist Resistance must rise from the despised depths. The CEO Donbo King Tyrump Presidency – that shit would have to be flushed away. This was the message that resonated every day and night through the Socialist analysis of President Tyrump's daily shit. This was the message that President Donbo King Tyrump, and his gun money handlers, knew he needed to destroy, at all costs.

III.

"Remember the Alamo!"

"Excuse me, Sir?"

President Tyrump smirked. "Dineh, do you remember that brilliant idea I came up with about invading Texas?"

"Vividly, Sir."

"Cowboys are my weakness, Dineh."

"Mr. President?"

"I would make a good Marlboro Man, don't

you think? Can you see me riding tall in a cowboy hat on a horse, Dineh? Like your people, right?"

"I thought Americans were my people, Sir."

"Don't push me, Dineh."

"Yes, Mr. President. Well, there has always been an uneasy relationship between cowboys and Natives. I do not think it will go well, Sir. Invading Texas."

"Texas can't wait, Dineh. We've got to build that wall to secure our good land, and our great money! So first things first. But we have a problem now that looks to be even bigger, the biggest one ever. And I am looking for a cowboy to fix it."

"A conquering cowboy, Sir?"

"This is a serious problem, Dineh."

"Climate change? Nuclear war?"

"You are too funny, Dineh. I can always count on you to lighten the mood around here. Everyone knows nothing can be done about the air, earth, and sky. Just like everyone knows nothing can be done about nuclear bombs. If they are going to go off, they are going to go off. You hope they go off over there and not over here..."

"But nuclear winter, Mr. President, the trade winds..."

"I'm not talking trade deals today, Dineh! Business is booming - for me and my kind - we only need to keep it going. Business has gotten everything it wants for decades! The banks even more, bloodsuckers that they are. I wish I were a banker, Dineh. Maybe someday. No, my fine man, I'm talking about the greatest political problem of our time confronting the One Percent of the One Percent, me and my kind. I'm talking about that goddamned- Oh, Hell! Look, Dineh! That thing! It's back!"

President Tyrump slapped the walnut desktop with both hands. Then he pointed at a spot 8 or 9 feet above the floor, above the coffee table in the middle of the Oval Office, directly below the Presidential Seal on the ceiling. There hovered a silent glowing object like a giant yellow pomelo, the largest of the citrus. It looked like a brilliant youth basketball, hovering in the air.

"Look at it! That terrible object! It's staring at us! Aiming!" said President Tyrump.

The silent Pomelo hovered, as if a levitating beautiful huge yellow fruit. It shimmered above the Oval Office coffee table.

"Is that not a goddamned drone?!" cried the President. "I'm the only one in the world who should be approving hit lists for drones blasting in other countries! Just like my inglorious predecessor Bars Bomba Obomba, executing throughout his term. This is no proper drone here! Why is it in my office, in the capitol of the world?! How does it hang before us as if we ourselves are a target?! Am I a goddamned sitting duck?! Answer me, Dineh! I know that hideous thing won't answer!" The brilliant orb gleamed.

"I'm sorry, Mr. President, the special Cabinet meeting is about to begin. Should we put it off?"

"The goddamned Cabinet! Those fools!" said

President Tyrump. "No, Dineh, let's have them stare down this drone face to...orb. Let's see what kind of guts my cabinet really has."

"As you wish, Sir."

"You know that these tools in my Cabinet are after only one thing, right, Dineh? Do you know what that thing is?"

"I would hesitate to guess, Sir. Money?"

"Power! They want my power! I am the greatest most powerful person in the world, and half of them want to carve me up and eat my body and drink my blood right out in public on the evening news. And they would do it if they could get away with it. They would rather rule the world each themselves. So, they are out to get me. They would see me impeached. My own Cabinet! They will try!"

"Yes, Sir, well the meeting is about to begin, Sir."

"Bloodsuckers," muttered President Tyrump.

The Vice President entered the Oval Office followed by most of the rest of the Cabinet and some leaders of Congress. For a moment a few of the officials continued to speak among themselves, while pointing and glancing uncertainly up at the hovering pomelo.

"Gentlemen, gentlewomen, please, sit," said President Tyrump.

The President smiled at the Cabinet and congressional leaders gathered before him very much the way a King Cobra smiles at its dinner in the weeds. The officials positioned themselves in front of the President's desk on decorative couches and ornamental chairs. They faced each other and President Tyrump across a coffee table upon which was set a silver bowl full of fake apples.

President Tyrump silenced the room by fixing the eyes of each Executing Officer.

The Pomelo glistened momentarily, then reverted to its usual bright glow.

"Goddamn it!" said President Tyrump. "What do we do about that horrible object?!"

The pomelo shimmered and bounced, levitating above the coffee table.

"Is that not a goddamned drone?!" said the President to the Cabinet. "Am I not the one supposed to be approving hit lists for drones blasting terrorists in other countries? That is no proper drone. Why is it in my office? How does it hang before us as if we ourselves are a goddamned target? Goddamn you all!"

"Call the cops!" suggested Vice President Rob Loot Thief. "We've been bugged! Targeted! Fruited!"

"Calm down, Loot Thief," said FBI Director, Payne Prison Police. "We are the cops."

"I'll kill it!" cried the Chairman of the Joint Chiefs, General Krushin Karvin Kilman rising toward the Pomelo, punching his right fist into his left palm.

"Hold off on that, Kilman," said CIA Director, Creepy Coupy Cutthroat. He grabbed the big General. "We don't know the thing's nature, origin, or manner of being."

"It's criminal whatever it is," said US

Attorney General, Lawkemup Libelem Lawless.

"Let me get my hands on it, I'll teach it a lesson," said the Secretary of Education, Shammi Shilling Sharlatan.

"It's a big fruit that pomelo!" shouted the Speaker of the House, Thuggy Thug Thuggun.

"It's a Communist fruit, I would bet on it," said the Director of the National Security Agency, Allsee Allhear Allspy. "It's probably from Communist Asia. Big pomelos there. This looks like the work of China. It's evil whatever it is. Come to battle the Good Guys. Well here we are."

"I wonder what it's worth," said the Secretary of the Treasury, Deadly Dollar Dealer. "I bet it would fetch a pretty penny underground."

"I'd buy it," said Congressional Senate Leader, Richi Rich Rich.

"Enough about the market value of the goddamned drone fruit!" cried President Donbo King Tyrump. "If anyone is going to buy or sell that thing, it's going to be me. But I would feel better if we could simply destroy it before it launches against us! So, what do we do now, my wise and noble team of experts?!"

"He makes fun of us, I believe," said Vice President Rob Loot Thief to CIA Director Creepy Coupy Cutthroat sitting beside him.

The President continued: "We haven't even been able to touch this thing since it first appeared a few days ago. We have no idea what it is, what it does, why it's here, where it's from. Have we been invaded? Is it extraterrestrial?

Alien? Did it cross the Rio Grande? Why can we not capture it? We know nothing. Have we tried everything? Anything?"

"Not everything," said CIA Director Creepy Coupy Cutthroat. "Rendition. We need to get it to a black site. There we'll learn the truth. We'll strip it naked and use wires and pliers. We've got drills, we've got fire. And water. And ice. For those who withhold the facts on the ground, we've got every way the world will end, right there in our shop. Torture can be a beautiful thing. If all else fails, we'll get out the nukes, gases, chemicals, and viral agents! We've got it all!"

The entire room stared at CIA Director Creepy Coupy Cutthroat.

"No offense, Creepy Coupy, but we may need to get you to a black site," said President Donbo King Tyrump.

CIA Director Cutthroat made a note on his handheld. "Very funny, Sir."

The Director of the National Security Agency Allsee Allhear Allspy ran a program on his own handheld that instantly hacked and decoded the note that Director Cutthroat was writing to himself, while he was writing it. NSA Director Allspy scowled and smacked Director Cutthroat on the shoulder. "No coups," he told him. "Not here. Not now, at least."

"I'm from New York, so pardon me, if I'm sensitive," said President Tyrump to CIA Director Cutthroat. "I prefer to live in my very own Tyrump Tower, and I don't want to see the world blown up beneath me. So cool it, Creepy Coupy. But don't get me wrong: if we can torture this yellow thing here in such a way that it won't lie to us, then be my guest. Just don't destroy the world in the meantime. Okay? Thanks, Coupy."

"Impossible," said Dineh. "Think about it. If anyone in this room were ever tortured, the first thing you would do is have a heart attack. The second thing you would do is tell your torturers whatever you think they want to hear. The truth would be irrelevent. People lie like mad to try to save themselves, whether they know anything or not. It's human nature. Plus it's completely monstrous."

"What are you trying to confess, Dineh?" said CIA Director Creepy Coupy Cutthroat.

"He's a mere aide," said NSA Director Allspy. "Ignore him." He pointed up at the Pomelo. "We don't understand its source of power. If we don't know that, we can't cut if off."

"We don't know who funds it," said Secretary of the Treasury Deadly Dollar Dealer.

"Hold on a minute," said FBI Director Payne Prison Police, tapping his smartphone. "I'll order the arrest of ten thousand people who might or might not know a thing."

"Make it twenty thousand," said CIA Director Creepy Coupy Cutthroat.

"Fifty thousand," commanded NSA Director Allsee Allhear Allspy.

"Do I hear one hundred?!" called Senate Leader Richi Rich Rich.

"We must force this drone to negotiate," said

the US Secretary of State, Oily Oily Oily. "I'll apply economic sanctions, and freeze its assets when we discover what and where they are. General, you might move the 4th Fleet into position. At least three aircraft carriers and plenty of submarines. What good is a mighty military if we don't use it? We can blast that pomelo to smithereens."

"I'm the President, remember?!" said President Donbo King Tyrump. "I give the orders around here, not you, Oily." The President sniffed audibly and wiped his nose. "Go ahead, General Kilman. Do whatever it takes."

"Should we really be targeting the Oval Office with the 4th Fleet?" asked Vice President Rob Loot Thief. "I'm sitting here, you know. Right here. We all are."

"Don't worry. They know what they're doing," said the Chairman of the Joint Chiefs, General Krushin Karvin Kilman.

"Guns are the answer. Trust me," said Speaker of the House, Thuggy Thug Thuggun.

"Can this thing even communicate?" asked President Tyrump. "Or does is merely spy and target, shoot first and ask questions later? Does it see, hear, smell? Can we blind it, drug it, deafen it? Can it be brainwashed? Made to go berserk? If not, how do we threaten it?"

"Do you speak English?! English!" shouted House Speaker Thuggy Thug Thuggun, at the pomelo. Then he declared to Attorney General Lawkemup Libelem Lawless: "By law this alien must speak English in the White House.

"There's no such law unfortunately, Thuggy," replied Attorney General Lawless. "Not to worry. I consider it legal to torture the thing, and spill its guts. Waterboard it, electrocute it, hang it upside down, pull a rope around its genitals..."

"It looks gender neutral to me," smirked House Speaker Thuggy Thug Thuggun.

At that moment, the Pomelo marked the forehead of President Tyrump with a bloody capital letter "A". The word "ASSASSIN" occasionally flashed in place of the single letter. And sometimes another word that began with "A". A dirty word. A shitty word.

The Cabinet gasped. President Donbo King Tyrump used his handheld as a mirror to inspect his forehead. "Holy Hell!" He ducked under the desk. The red letter A then glowed on the desktop marking exactly the spot beneath which the President endeavored to hide.

General Kilman drew his saber from the holster of his dress uniform and tried to stab and slash at the Pomelo above. He may as well have knifed a hologram. Nor did the General's attack interrupt the imprinting of the President with the bloody letter A.

No one noticed CIA Director Creepy Coupy Cutthroat slip away, until he returned and tried to capture the Pomelo in a clear glass of water. He stepped onto the coffee table and capped the top of a glass with a binder of disinformation notes, to no discernible effect. The Pomelo shimmered through the water and continued to brand the President with the bloody letter A.

"Coupy, what the hell? Is that some kind of water torture?" asked Senate Leader Richi Rich Rich.

"This thing is real," said CIA Director Creepy Coupy Cutthroat. "For a minute there, I thought it might be one of our own hologram drones gone awry, astray, AWOL. But this one has no identifying marks."

"Wait a minute." Via his handheld, NSA Director Allsee Allhear Allspy turned off the lights in the Oval Office, thinking the Drone might be an optical illusion. The Pomelo gleamed brighter, spearing the President's head with the bloody letter A. Director Allspy's efforts caused the lights to flicker before power was fully restored. "Time to upgrade this thing," he said, tapping his handheld.

"Goddamn it!" shouted the Speaker of the House, Thuggy Thug Thuggun. He ripped his shoe off his right foot, then flung it at the Pomelo. The shoe sailed through the air, bounced off the granite bust of Martin Luther King and smashed through a collection of Native American pottery.

"Good shot, Thuggy," said FBI Director Payne Prison Police.

President Donbo King Tyrump clambered back onto his chair and sat disconsolate, a marked man. He stared at the shattered Native American pottery. "Don't worry, Thuggy," he said. "There's more where that came from. Right, Dineh? You will be happy, House Speaker Thuggun, to replace it for me."

Attorney General Lawkemup Libelem Lawless held his smartphone near the Pomelo in a non-legalistic attempt to shield President Donbo King Tyrump from the branding of the pomelo. No effect. The bloody letter "A" seemed permanently inscribed upon the President.

A grim silence gripped the Oval Office.

"Where's Press Secretary Bullcrap Baloney Bullshat? He can talk to anyone to no end. Get him in here to talk to this thing! Where is Bullshat?!"

"He's out sick, Sir. Laryngitis."

"That figures! Our speaker can't speak!"

"I'm the only Speaker around here!" said Thuggy Thug Thuggun. "I always knew Bullshat's vocal cords would reject him sooner or later, the way he likes to reject my brilliant ideas for social order! No offense, Mr. President."

"Plenty taken!" said President Tyrump. "Are you a Drone?" asked the President of the Pomelo. "Are you a Socialist? Are you with the Resistance?"

"The Drone is a Socialist?!" cried General Krushin Karvin Kilman. "I thought the drones were on our side!"

"It's the End of the World as we know it," moaned Vice President Rob Loot Thief.

"No yellow drone will take away my right to bear arms!" shouted House Speaker Thuggun. He pulled out a fully working plastic pistol that he had smuggled past the metal detectors and the Secret Service, and he pointed it at the drone. The drone glittered briefly. "I've got you now!"

said House Speaker Thuggun.

"There will be trouble if video of this gets out," said Attorney General Lawkemup Libelem Lawless. "Everyone, turn off your handhelds." No one did, including the Attorney General.

"Kill the Drone!" shouted US House Speaker Thuggun standing on one shoe and waving his little plastic gun.

Suddenly upon the center of US House Speaker Thuggun's forehead glistened the phosphorescent image of the buttocks of an enormous man.

In panic, all the Executing Officers of the US Cabinet used the reflective surfaces of their handhelds to examine their own foreheads.

"You get the hell down!" screamed Vice President Rob Loot Thief at the Pomelo.

"You have the right to remain silent!" shouted FBI Director Payne Prison Police. "Anything you say can and will be used against you in a court of law. You have the right to speak to an attorney, and to have an attorney present, during any questioning. If you are rendered to a black site, none of this applies. We will do with you as we please in any prison, anywhere, goddamn it! Now get down from there! I order you to surrender!"

"Go to hell," said the Pomelo.

"It talks!" shouted President Tyrump.

The Vice President fouled his pants. The stench permeated the room. He slunk out.

"Vice President Rob Loot Thief is not the only one among you who is completely full of shit," said the Pomelo.

"Wait, who are you?" said Attorney General Lawkemup Libelem Lawless suspiciously.

"I think I recognize the voice!" said Secretary of Education Shammi Shilling Sharlatan. "It's What's-His-Name!"

"What's-his-name?!"

"Who's What's-His-Name?!"

"It's What's-His-Name! What's-His-Name!"

"Holy Shit, shut up!" yelled President Tyrump.

"Somebody speak English!" cried US House Speaker Thuggy Thug Thuggun.

"Who on Earth?! What's-His-Name?!" asked General Kilman.

"I think I know exactly who you are," said Attorney General Lawless. He tapped rapidly on his handheld.

"I'm Justice Assured. Of Wikilooks."

"I'll handle this," said CIA Director Creepy Coupy Cuttthroat. "It's time to call Wikilooks what it really is: A hostile spy agency often aligned with enemy states like Russia."

"It's time to call the CIA what it is," said Justice Assured of Wikilooks. "The CIA is the world's most notorious state terrorist agency, currently drone bombing to death civilians overseas on a regular basis. And the President in the White House is the hands-on boss of the Director of the CIA."

President Donbo King Tyrump fainted. He slid out of his chair, knocked his head on the desk, and thudded onto the floor.

"How may we be of assistance?" asked US Senate Leader Richi Rich Rich opening his arms wide to the Pomelo. "I'm sure that we can come to some mutually rewarding arrangement."

"How dare you!" House Leader Thuggy Thug Thuggun leveled his plastic handgun and shot Senate Leader Richi Rich Rich in the chest. He would later claim, "on accident" and that he had been aiming at the drone pomelo.

Then US House Speaker Thuggun raised his pistol and actually did aim at the pomelo, firing a shot that passed through to no effect except that the pomelo shimmered and sparkled. The bullet ripped through the Presidential Seal on the ceiling.

Finally Speaker Thuggun leveled the gun at the marble bust of Martin Luther King and fired a shot that ricocheted off the marble and struck Presidential Aide Dineh in the thigh. Dineh fell back against the Oval Office wall.

US Joint Chiefs General Krushin Karvin Kilman tackled House Speaker Thuggun and thumped him onto the floor.

NSA Director Allsee Allhear Allspy sent a warning note to every satellite in orbit that the White House was under assault, possibly by the Russians or the Chinese or the Iranians or jihadis.

All the other Executing Officers in the room either froze in place or threw themselves on the floor.

A group of Secret Service agents rushed into the room. Dineh, as nearly the only person of color in the Oval Office with an untold number of armed white men, raised his hands and said, "Don't shoot! I've already been shot!"

Dineh was tackled and rammed against the wall. "I can't breathe!" he managed in a brief moment when he could force out any words.

"Where have I heard that before?" said the Secret Service agent pinning him to the wall. "Why did you shoot the Senator, you criminal?!"

"Wasn't me!"

"Thought you said you couldn't breathe!"

"Can't! Not in!" Dineh passed out still pinned upright against the wall.

The Secret Service agents swarming the room surrounded the President unconscious on the floor.

The mob of agents was so overwhelming that as more flooded in they accidentally knocked aside the agent choking Dineh, who dropped to the floor.

When Dineh regained consciousness, he found himself ignored. He crawled along the wall away from the scrum of agents around the President. Dineh left a trail of blood and some tears on the polished wood floor beyond the edge of the rug. In a more calm spot, he probed his leg for the bullet. A flesh wound. Dineh used the wall to pull himself up and found he could stand and survey the scene. Panicked agents prodded the prone President Tyrump and yelled at their radios.

Dineh put both hands into the air again. "I've got this! I've got this!" he hollered, hobbling away from the wall, hands held high, toward President Tyrump. "The President needs his medicine! The medicine! I'm the one who gives him the medicine! It's there in the desk!"

The Secret Service agents grudgingly let Dineh limp through their gauntlet of guns, hands up.

"One wrong move, and you're toast, Brownie," a Secret Service agent threatened Dineh.

Finally, Dineh reached the presidential desk where he tapped in the code to unlock the special compartment. His coding in seemed to impress the agents who gave Dineh a little more space to work. Probably some of the agents were relieved to have someone else to blame for President Tyrump's death, should he pass.

Dineh squirted the liquid magic into the nostrils of President Tyrump and watched for an effect.

After a moment, President Tyrump appeared to smile weakly but remained unconscious.

US Senate Leader Richi Rich Rich lay bleeding on the other side of the President's desk in the center of the Oval Office. A few agents worked his wounds and called for water.

Nearby, also on the floor, General Krushin Karvin Kilman had all but detached the arms from the body of House Speaker Thuggy Thug Thuggun, whose limbs were wrapped behind his back in a pretzel of impossible angles, tied up with the belt of General Kilman. Speaker Thuggun appeared to have passed out. At least, he wasn't speaking.

"Come on, Mr. President, wake up now. Just another day at the office." Dineh rocked the President and shook him lightly. Then he reached for a second bottle of nasal spray.

Dineh wondered why the Secret Service agents were pressing in tight again, until he noticed that the room had filled with even more agents, a number of whom seemed to be working furiously on some problem near each of the four entrances to the Oval Office.

Dineh's leg throbbed. An ominous feeling swept through him. This can't be good, Dineh thought, as he slipped another bottle into a nostril of the President.

"You're killing me, Dineh!" This was how President Donbo Tyrump recovered from knocking himself out on the desk.

Dineh quickly pulled the bottle of nasal spray from the nose of the President, who flailed about. Dineh backed off as quickly as he could. Not quick enough. Dineh was hoisted by a Secret Service agent, dragged off, and then flung against the wall of the Oval Office. Dineh congratulated himself on not getting tased.

"What the filch is going on?!" Propped up on his feet, disoriented, and feeling threatened, President Donbo King Tyrump lashed out with a wild punch, a desperate right hook, into the gut of the Secret Service agent who had helped him up.

The punch had no effect upon the agent, other than to cause him to let go of the President, who wobbled but managed to remain upright on his own.

"What the hell happened around here?" The President squinted up at the pomelo. "You!" he shouted. "You devil! You caused all this!"

"Actually, Sir," said CIA Director Creepy Coupy Cutthroat, sidling up to the center of power. "House Speaker Thuggun shot Senate Leader Rich with a smuggled pistol. Richi may live, he may not."

"I'll live!" shouted Senate Leader Richi Rich Rich from the blood-soaked floor.

"That remains to be seen," said FBI Director Payne Prison Police to the President. "Speaker Thuggun also shot the pomelo, to no effect, a pity. Then Speaker Thuggun tagged the marble bust of Martin Luther King. We don't know what got in to him. It's as if he lost his sense of history."

"MLK! Christ!" President Donbo King Tyrump gazed through the throng, taking in the chaotic scene, trying to make sense of it all. "And what happened to me, Director?!"

"You fainted, hit your head," said FBI Director Payne Prison Police.

"Dineh over there brought you back. I don't trust him," said CIA Director Cutthroat.

"Relax, Coupy," said NSA Director Allspy. "Now is not the time."

Someone appeared to be in charge of the many security agents crowding the office but President Donbo King Tyrump had no idea who. "You!" he shouted again at the pomelo. "You caused my Senate Leader to get shot! You killed him!"

"I'm okay, I'll be okay," gasped Senate Leader Richi Rich Rich.

"Shut up, Richi! One problem at a time!" said President Tyrump.

"It was that guy!" Senator Leader Richi Rich Rich pointed weakly at US House Speaker Thuggy Thug Thuggun. "He shot me!"

"On accident! I swear!" said Speaker Thuggun, who appeared to be alive and conscious after all, beneath the tangled mess of his arms broken behind his back by General Kilman. "I was aiming at that thing!" He pointed with his bloody nose up at the bright glowing pomelo.

"You'll pay for this!" said Senate Leader Richi Rich Rich to House Speaker Thuggy Thug Thuggun.

"We are all going to pay for this, I have a feeling," said President Donbo King Tyrump, unaware in the moment how terribly right he was.

"Mr. President," interrupted NSA Leader Allsee Allhear Allspy, "remember when you ordered the 4th Fleet to target the pomelo here in the Oval Office, shortly before you fainted and knocked yourself unconscious?"

"The talking pomelo startled me," said the President. "Yes, I remember. So what?"

"The 4th Fleet does not have a weapon that can target and destroy the pomelo without also destroying the entire city of Washington DC," said Director Allspy.

"Tell me something I don't know, Director. No one knows exactly what will destroy the pomelo. The point was to try to scare it, and to defend against it, not to destroy the capital city. Which would be, you know, insane, right?"

"I understand, Sir. However, the Fourth Fleet felt compelled to follow your orders, Sir." NSA Director Allspy glanced at his handheld. "The Fleet targeted the Oval Office, Sir."

"That shows they know who is in charge, Allspy. Me! Donbo King Tyrump. I am their ultimate commander, the President. I am the commander in chief of the US armed forces," said President Donbo King Tyrump. "So what?"

"Yes, Sir. Perhaps they assumed that the Oval Office had been taken over. Anyway, I suppose it's not their fault, Mr. President. Sir, the Commander of the Fourth Fleet, Rear Admiral Bunkie Bilgie Bentcan has informed me directly, Sir - upon learning that the Chairman of the Joint Chiefs General Krushin Karvin Kilman was currently indisposed, securing House Speaker Thuggy Thug Thuggun, Sir - that one of the Fourth Fleet's nuclear submarines has been hacked, Sir. As a consequence, a nuclear ballistic missile has been launched, Sir, a Trident II. It will destroy everything here in Washington DC. It will arrive..." - NSA Director Allspy checked his handheld again - "...in 15 minutes, Sir. It will strike the Oval Office. It will destroy the entire city."

"Come again, Allspy? A US submarine

Trident missile? Hacked? Launched? A nuclear bomb? Like Hiroshima? Launched by whom?!"

"Much worse, Sir. Much, much worse. The submarine carries 24 missiles, Sir. One Trident II missile was launched and targeted at the Oval Office. That missile has four nuclear warheads that could be targeted at four different targets, like fingers of God, but instead these four have all been targeted here, at the Oval Office, Sir, and each of these four nuclear warheads on this missile is thirty times more powerful than the nuclear bomb that destroyed Hiroshima, Japan. That power is going to destroy Washington DC, and then some."

"But that's insane!"

"I'm sorry, Sir."

"Well, shoot it down!"

"Impossible, Sir."

"Then, disable it!"

"These missiles are designed to not be disabled. Anyone could do so, if they were. These missiles cannot be stopped nor destroyed before reaching the target. This missile will detonate immediately above this office and destroy this city. Washington DC is gone, Sir. I'm sorry."

"What the filch?! You're 'sorry'?! You destroyed this city, you killed us all, the leader of the free world, me, and you're 'sorry', Director Allspy?!"

"I did not hack the missile, Sir!"

"I'm glad to hear that, Director! Who did?! Goddamn it! Who hacked the nukes?! The Russians?! The Chinese?! My wife?! Some punk sixteen year old in Australia?! Who?! The Chinese are killing us! Was it them?!"

"It was the Texans, Sir."

"The filch!!! The Texans?! Our Texans?!"

"The Texans, of Texas, USA. Yes, Sir. The Great Texas Republic Fundamentalist Independence Group, Sir. That's what they call themselves. The US National Security Agency has been battling the secessionists along with the illegals for many years now. Apparently the Texas Fundies believe that you, Mr. President, are attacking Texas, Sir. The Texas Fundies are a people of great belief, Sir. Terrorists, true. And great believers."

"We are building the Great Wall of Texas, Director! The gas and oil prices have dropped but will come back up, I'm told! We've got to build that wall! The Texas Fundies, and their like, we were counting on them as allies not enemies! What a humongous mix-up!"

"Yes, Sir." NSA Director Allspy referred to his handheld. "Well, Sir, the Great Texas Republic Fundamentalist Independence Group has issued a statement to the media claiming that they are destroying Washington DC as an act of self defense. They claim that you, Sir, are perpetrating an act of great terror, an invasion of Texas. They believe this, Sir. Or possibly it is some group posing as the Texas Fundies, Sir. It is too late to advise them of their error, if error it is, whoever they may be! They say you left them no recourse, Sir."

"The filch!" said the President. "How is it

possible that nuclear weapons can be hacked?! You can't have nuclear weapons that can be hacked, Director!"

"They are not my weapons, Sir. They are his." Director Allspy pointed at General Kilman kneeling on the back of House Speaker Thuggun. "And they are your weapons, Mr. President."

"I don't care whose weapons they are, Director Allspy! If someone, anyone, can hack, launch, and destroy whoever they want, or the part of the world they hate, or fear, or mistakenly target, then what the Hell?!"

"What the Hell, indeed, Sir."

"If the computers can be fooled, the systems rigged, or the launch personnel tricked, then no one is safe anywhere at anytime ever!"

"No, Sir. Certainly not us," said Director Allspy.

Like most people in the room, Dineh had moved close to the intense discussion being held at the President's desk. "Sir, no one was ever safe with nuclear weapons. Computer systems malfunction from time to time. The world was nearly blown up repeatedly these past decades." Dineh was now standing near the President. "If there is nuclear retaliation to this bombing of DC and if enough bombs go off," said Dineh, "then the subsequent nuclear winters will destroy all the rest of the world, even the parts the bombers may love."

"What world are we living in?" asked the President.

"Your world, Sir. Our world. Whose else?

These are electronic computerized systems operated by potentially fallible personnel," explained Director Allsee Allhear Allspy. "All such systems can be breached, hacked, taken over, tricked, or controlled remotely. Or they can simply malfunction. The National Security Council and the armed forces have done everything in their powers for years to prevent this, Sir. At least once a decade from the start of the nuclear age, accidental computer glitches and malfunctions have caused both the US and Russia to think they were under imminent nuclear attack. Fortunately disaster was narrowly avoided each time by some gutsy and risky decision making at different levels. People had to guess at what was really going on with the computers. And guess correctly. Unfortunately, there is no uncertainty this time. Multiple sources confirm, Sir. And immediate eye-witnesses. This one got away from us, Sir. These Texan crazies are not under our control. It has happened, Sir. I am sorry."

"Filch you, Director! You're as crazy as the Texas crazies! I'll bet you are from Texas!" shouted the President.

"I did not bomb myself, Sir."

"I think you did! You may as well have! I think this whole nuclear weapons system itself is crazy since it can be set off by mistake, or by goddamn hacking! Our fate is in the hands of filching terror gamers!"

"It long has been," said Dineh. "We've been incredibly lucky to make it this far. It's a miracle we're alive now."

"Well so much for that brief moment! If what you are saying is true, Director Allspy, then the only way to keep from getting blown up by nuclear weapons is to get rid of them in the first place!" said the President.

"That's true," said Dineh. "If nuclear weapons are not abolished, then we will all die by nuclear weapons one day, sooner or later. You can't keep getting lucky forever. It's statistically impossible. We'll all be killed, either by accident or on purpose, the world, the planet, the globe, everyone will someday be killed by nuclear bombardment, and by the atmosphere-collapsing aftermath, unless we get rid of the nukes. All of them. We'll all be killed by the blasts, by the radiation fallout, by the fires, or by nuclear winter. Everyone. Nuclear winter will kill almost all creatures large and small, everywhere. Maybe all. All humans will die."

"What in God's name is 'nuclear winter'?" asked the President.

NSA Director Allsee Allhear Allspy explained quickly: "Firestorms set off by dozens, let alone hundreds or thousands, of nuclear blasts would throw enough soot and smoke into the air to block out ninety-nine percent of the sun, for years. Needless to say, no civilization would survive. The entire human species would be snuffed out entirely."

"Don't forget," said House Speaker Thuggy Thug Thuggun from the floor, "this may be the Lord our God's Divine Plan."

"Filch you, Thuggun!" said the President. "If nuclear obliteration is in fact the Lord your God's plan, then the Lord your God is a complete sicko. It certainly seems to be the 'Divine Plan' of the Texas Fundies!"

"God is no sicko, Mr. President! How dare you?!" said House Speaker Thuggy Thug Thuggun.

"Your God is make-believe," said Justice Assured via the pomelo to House Speaker Thuggun. "All Gods are make-believe. I'm sorry. That's reality. No Gods, no masters. No masters, the goal. No Gods, the reality."

"Does anyone else have any more happy thoughts they would like to share with the group before we are all blown to pieces?!" said President Donbo King Tyrump. "Are you all from Neptune?!" screamed President Donbo King Tyrump. "I thought I was the most likely candidate for lunacy around here when I ran my crazy election campaign, my kooky carnival for the pimp media! But now I learn that I'm not even close to the loony bin compared to you oh so respectable executing officers! How in the world did I get elected to this godforsaken place! It turns out that you executing officials who control the goddamned nuclear weapons are even crazier than I am! I just wanted to make more money, Honey! And feel more power! I never wanted to kill off the entire world! Okay, so, I suppose I did not quite care who lived or who died. I never really wanted to think about it. But who would have thought that any group of loose hacker nuts could incinerate the whole planet if they chose to?!"

"Climate change is torching the planet too," said Justice Assured via the pomelo. "If the Texas Fundies and the nukes didn't get you, climate change would be coming for you too. Nukes, climate change. Different timeframes. Maybe. It's tough to figure," said Justice Assured. "Either way, it's the road to total Hell. Whatever your idea of Hell, climate collapse or nukes are sure ways to get there."

"The road to Hell?!" said President Tyrump. "I'm beginning to think we're sitting at the very center of Hell right here!"

"That would make you the Devil, Sir," said CIA Director Creepy Coupy Cutthroat.

"And you the Devil's idiot mole!" said the President.

NSA Director Allsee Allhear Allspy tapped his handheld. "Don't worry, Mr. President. I've alerted every country with nuclear weapons that we have bombed ourselves, so that they won't think we may mistakenly retaliate against them with our nuclear arsenal. I hope they believe us, so that they don't launch a mistaken pre-emptive strike our way."

"Well filch you!" said the President. "No need to worry then! You've got it all under control, Allspy! Right up to the point where we go up in a cloud of radioactive smoke!"

"It's true, the other nuclear powers may get nervous and nuke the rest of the country out of fear," continued Director Allspy. "How can they be sure what's going on? But it's the best we can do, now. I've alerted all our nuclear commanders as well about the fate of DC, so that they do not think we are under attack from abroad and launch God knows where in retaliation. I hope they understand and make no moves to launch. We definitely don't want the Russians to panic and launch their big arsenal. Or the Israelis. Or the Pakistanis. Or anyone. Cooler heads have prevailed in the past. We can take comfort in that."

"Oh what a relief!" the President spat at the NSA Director. "It takes only one mistake to destroy everything. One loss of temper. One goddamned hacker! So don't worry about giant stockpiles of nuclear weapons just lying around, primed to launch, waiting to be filching hacked or mistakenly set off! We have systems and protocols for that! Security galore! If I had it in my real power, I would destroy you all right now before the goddamn nukes do!"

"You don't mean that, Sir. We are all under a lot of stress here."

"Stress? Director, are you referring to the unavoidable fact of immediate obliteration?! Then yes, we are undergoing a bit of a trial at the moment. You filching idiot!"

"Our nuclear commanders are conferring as we speak. The military can handle this, Sir."

"Clearly, the military can handle it. What was I thinking? It has done such a bang-up job to this point, keeping us safe! No lives lost around here. Not at the moment!

"Yes, Sir."

"Oh, and by the way, Director Allspy and General Kilman and Director Cutthroat and the rest of you morons, good job on 9-11. Keeping us safe. You really did a bang-up job there!"

"Sir, that was before our time," said NSA Director Allspy.

"Oh, no, I don't think it was, Director. It seems to be totally of your time. And now you will add the vaporization of the capital of America to your fine efforts!"

"That's on all of you," said Justice Assured. "9-11. And so are these nukes. 9-11 was a monstrous retaliation for your monstrous imperialism in western Asia, what you call the Middle East, and beyond. Who here denies that, by now?"

"It wasn't my fault!" said President Tyrump. "I was building resorts, hotels, golf courses, restaurants, fish ponds."

"Fish ponds, Sir?" said Dineh.

"People like fish, Dineh!"

"Be that as it may, Mr. President," said NSA Director Allspy, "Fourth Fleet Rear Admiral Bunkie Bilgie Bentcan reports that his intelligence officers believe that the hack has been limited to the one submarine and to only the one missile on that submarine."

"Oh, they '*believe*', do they, Allspy? Well, thank God for belief! But do they *know*?"

"Yes, Sir. I believe so, Sir. I mean ... I mean merely one of twenty-four nuclear ballistic missiles on that sub has been launched against us, Sir. A nearly perfect record! Unfortunately, that one missile does contain multiple nuclear warheads of immense power, as I mentioned. That missile is the one that got away. A pity. The only one."

It was at this precise moment that the President of the United States of America, Donbo King Tyrump, tried to kill NSA Director Allsee Allhear Allspy. The President grabbed the Director around the throat with both hands and attempted to cut off the air and blood to his brain.

CIA Director Creepy Coupy Cutthroat and FBI Director Payne Prison Police grabbed the President each by an arm and pulled him back from NSA Director Allsee Allhear Allspy and restrained the President where he stood.

"Okay, you idiots, let me go!" said the President.

The two executing officers merely eased their grip.

"One missile is not such a bad number, I suppose, Director Allspy," said the President. "Until you realize that one missile with its multiple warheads can destroy multiple cities at once. Such a trivial fact. You colossal brain suck!"

"The sub is quite powerful, Sir."

"All of its warheads are aimed at this office? I have family in other cities."

"We all do, Sir. Fortunately. Yes, I'm told that each of the warheads on this missile is aimed at the Oval Office, Sir. That is, at you. Of course, everything from the Atlantic Ocean to

Hagerstown, Maryland will be radioactive, Sir. And beyond. But we don't need to worry about the rest of the US at the moment, I think. Much of the radiation should drift out to sea, if the wind picks up, and then scatter across Europe."

"Oh, lucky them. Thanks for that huge dose of comfort and consolation, Director Allspy. I'll try not to worry too much before we are incinerated, and the city is torched, and the whole region is poisoned. How much time do we have left?"

"Ten minutes."

"Outstanding. Ten minutes. Condemned to spend it with all you absolute Losers."

The CIA and FBI Directors let go of the President's arms now that he had returned to his senses.

The Chairman of the Joint Chiefs General Krushin Karvin Kilman shoved off from House Speaker Thuggy Thug Thuggun who was tied up and no longer ambulatory.

"How do you suppose the stock market will react?" asked the Secretary of the Treasury Deadly Dollar Dealer.

"You know it will shoot sky high at some point soon," said Oily Oily Oily, the Secretary of State. "Wars and big military spending tend to have that effect. Guns are good for gold."

"I wish I could reach my broker right now," said Senate Leader Richi Rich Rich, flat on the floor.

General Krushin Karvin Kilman stepped into the tight tense circle of power. "I couldn't help but overhear," he said. "Is it true? We are about to be blasted to smithereens?"

"Yes, by your military!" said the President. "One of your missiles, General, simply slipped through your fingers. Outstanding job, General. You'll certainly pay for that. We all will. It was the Texans who got the best of you, General. You're not Texan, are you General? I know that so many of you military types are. One of your buddies perhaps? Many Texas Fundies in the military, General? I think we all know the answer to that. Loose lips used to sink ships, General. Now apparently it's loose cannons who can blow up entire capital cities of the world!"

"We are in a bit of a pickle," said NSA Director Allspy.

Once again the President needed to be blocked from attacking the NSA Director.

"Hold on," said General Kilman, stopping the fight, for a change, before it began. "What are we waiting for? Let's all go into the bunker immediately, the underground command and control post below the Oval Office, right here. Let's go!" Joint Chiefs General Krushin Karvin Kilman pointed at the floor. "It's dozens of feet underground and designed to withstand a direct nuclear strike. We can ride this thing out. We can save ourselves and strike back against the Texans!"

"Damn straight!" said President Tyrump. "That's what I wanted all along! What are we thinking?! Why are we thinking?! Let's move!"

"Sir," said NSA Director Allsee Allhear Allspy,

"I'm sorry, Sir, we can't. We can't do any of that. I'm sorry."

"You're goddamn right you're sorry, Allspy! Why in God's name not?! Why can't we go into the bunker?!"

"The Texas Fundies not only hacked the nuclear submarine, Sir, they hacked the Oval Office. We are locked in, I'm sorry, Sir. Look around. You see Secret Service agents at each exit trying to break out. It's impossible. The Oval Office was retrofitted this past year. No one can break in. And we've been jammed. No one can get out. We are now trapped in an oval vessel, an oval seal."

"We have returned to the egg," said Dineh. "We have been returned to the egg by lunatics. By our own hands. By officialdom."

NSA Director Allspy ignored Dineh. "The walls, floor, and ceiling are lined and webbed with concrete and steel," said Director Allspy. "The windows here behind your desk, Mr. President, are bullet proof, shatter proof, blast proof, impregnable. The special escape door to the bunker is sealed. The biometric information required to break these seals has been hacked, altered, scrambled. There is no physical nor electronic way into here, and there is now no physical nor electronic way out. Only a direct nuclear blast can break the seals. And that blast will kill us all, Sir. Again, I do apologize."

"God damn you, Allspy! If you aren't the most useless criminal know-it-all around here, I don't know who is! Or what you are! My God!

You're Death with a handheld!" Then the President looked at General Kilman. "And you!" The President glanced around. "And you! And you! And you! All of you!"

"Look in the mirror," said Justice Assured.

"My vote is for Thuggun!" gasped Senate Leader Richi Rich Rich. "He's the Devil too! He fired the first shot!"

"If they hacked us in here," said General Krushin Karvin Kilman, "can we not hack our way out?"

NSA Director Allspy glanced at his handheld. "We are working on it, General. It can be done of course. There is a problem. It may take several hours. It will take more time than we have."

"We are caught in our own cage!" screamed President Tyrump. "A deep underground bunker beneath us and we can't even enter it! Brilliant! I knew I should have stuck with building casinos, bars, and hotels! Financial conquest is all I ever wanted! Screw military empire! How much time do we have now, Allspy?!"

"Eight minutes, Sir."

"Eight minutes left with you complete Losers! Who could have planned it better?! I blame you, Pomelo!" The President shouted at the glowing bright orb. "I blame you, Justice Assured! You and Wikilooks!"

"This madness, we tried to stop it many times over. Wikilooks and many others, we tried," replied Justice Assured. "We tried to stop you suicidal officials and pathological executives with your insane violent systems destroying so many people, destroying the planet, set to auto-destruct. Exactly as you have sown, now do you reap. We put everything we had into trying to stop your insane...everything."

"Well you too will be blasted, when the nukes hit!"

"Not for now, not this time," said Justice Assured via the pomelo. "So far, I've managed to keep away from Washington DC. You all have done your best, or I should say your very worst, to try to capture me, tie me up, and drag me there to you. This pomelo is a mirage of sorts. A truth-telling, truth-revealing kind of mirage."

"Goddamn you!" screamed the President.

"You have all brought oblivion onto yourselves. There's not much left to see here," said Justice Assured.

"There may be one thing," said Dineh, to no one in particular. "I can think of one thing."

"Well, what is it, Dineh?!" said President Tyrump. "Think fast, man, think fast!"

IV.

In earlier days, during better times, in the first few weeks of his glorious presidency, when the worst that President Donbo King Tyrump had been forced to deal with was the sewer of his own shit echoing in his ears, President Tyrump had tried everything within his powers to stop the infernal Socialist analysis of his daily shit. This was the great problem of his time, as he and the ruling class saw it. The shitty situation was so dire that President Donbo King Tyrump called an emergency meeting of the six other rulers of the world, the CEO President Kings of China, Europe, India, Russia, Oceania, and Africa. They too were under Socialist attack, constant toilet bowl analysis of each King's daily shit. Shit-rakers gone viral, an unholy shit-storm gone beast mode: an intolerable breach of etiquette, this was what the rulers of the world vowed to crush.

"This shit uprising is a planet-wide insurrection that must be put the fokkk down!" declared Donbo King Tyrump to his fellow rulers.

"You control the lands, air, seas, and space," said ChinaKing to AmeriKing. "What do you suggest?"

The seven Kings of Dearth agreed to convene, to try to reassert control and discipline upon the world. AmericaKing Tyrump presumed to be King for both Americas, North and South, and refused to allow noble SouthAmeriKing to attend the convention.

The Kings built a fortified floating island at a secret spot on the Pacific Ocean. "Conquerors Island," the Socialists named the phony giant lily pad and broadcast the precise GPS coordinates once it was at last complete. Resistance drones were welcome, but the Socialists encouraged flesh-and-blood people to stay away from the island given the extreme degree of insanity and high tech weaponry found there, all the while planing 24/7 live drone coverage of the proceedings.

And proceed the Kings did no matter the blown secrecy, formerly known as security. The Kings motorized the island and moved it about the Pacific in a vain attempt to lose the Socialists. The only result was that the meeting needed to be postponed a day when IndiaKing and his retinue were unable to locate the conference.

The Socialists attempted to assist IndiaKing by providing the correct vectors to the shifting island. IndiaKing ignored the Socialists and thus suffered the mortal embarrassment of having ChinaKing finally show up on the open seas to lead IndiaKing to the meeting.

As with President Donbo King Tyrump, the other Kings of the world had been forced to listen to their twice daily rectal symphonies globally broadcast by the popular forces of the Resistance and Socialists in their own lands. No wonder then that the Kings met as far as possible between these dawn and dusk inescapable embarrassments of the official orifices, at High Noon.

At that time, they paraded upon the Pacific: AmeriKing, ChinaKing, EuroKing, IndiaKing, RussiaKing, OceaniaKing, and AfriKing, the Lords who dominated Dearth all but unchecked prior to the rise of the Resistance and the Socialists. The seven Kings of Earth become Dearth become D'Empire.

"Never has a more repellent group gathered in one spot," reported the Socialists in dispassionate appraisal.

"We come in peace," the Kings announced to one another, without laughing, on their self-appointed self-anointed day.

And then once again, the Socialist's bright glowing yellow drone pomelo appeared, hovering close above Conquerors Island. Chaos erupted.

All manner of weaponry unleashed itself against the pomelo to no effect.

In the madness, EuroKing was jostled and bumped toward the edge of the island and the shark-filled Pacific. Every other King had motive. Some more than others. None claimed credit. EuroKing tried to save himself but slipped and flailed into the Pacific. The waters frothed. Fins danced. Further official hysteria ensued.

The pomelo shone more brightly than ever before.

In the end, EuroKing lost Italy to the snacking sharks: one entire leg and a boot. More than a few Sicilians were heard to laugh. EuroKing was hauled thrashing and screaming back onto Conquers Island by an attendant Loyal Debtor.

Then a giant shark convulsed and threw up the leg onto Conquerors Island like some wretched missile from the depths. It knocked over AfriKing who crashed onto the circular conference table and lay immobile, concussed, EuroKing's detached boot on his neck.

AmeriKing grabbed the broken body of AfriKing and flung him off the table to land with a thud. Then EuroKing was slid onto the table, where a great surgeon, the personal physician traveling with ChinaKing, worked to reattach EuroKing's severed leg. The surgeon did what he could and got the limb and boot reconnected to the body of EuroKing, except backwards. Too late, EuroKing wished that he had paid for his own medical retainers.

A couple billion Chinese laughed, getting a real kick out of the ostensible mistake. ChinaKing remarked that a crooked boot and slight limp was a small price to pay for swimming with sharks.

Possibly no one noticed the botched leg-saving surgery because AmeriKing insisted that the meeting resume with the surgery ongoing on the conference table.

AmeriKing called for military action against the strongholds of the Socialists, that is, direct against most households globally.

EuroKing voted prostrate in the affirmative.

OceaniaKing could not stop staring, having never seen EuroKing struck so low. Certain ideas began to occur to OceaniaKing whose people had suffered for centuries under the lash of the Dutch East India Company and who still struggled with heavy European baggage. OceaniaKing's realm of rule was nothing if not surrounded by sharks. He thought EuroKing might better limp carefully around Oceania upon any future travels.

A final vote was taken.

The unanimous decision surprised no one: the Kings agreed to first obliterate the

Resistance, and then to imprison or to inescapably indebt every last Socialist, and in fact for good measure to more deeply indebt nearly every person on Dearth.

A great cheer went up around the King's conference table in the Pacific.

AmeriKing CEO President Tyrump stood up and declared: "Kings of the World, your duty here is complete. Now return to your Kingdoms and conquer well!"

There was only one problem.

The pomelo had disabled their crafts. Nothing worked. No communications equipment, no computers. Nothing moved. No planes, no helicopters, no boats. The Kings of the World were stuck on Conquerors Island.

Fireworks erupted across Dearth exploding every computer chip in every weapon, in every weapons system, and in every military computer in the world. Fireworks erupted in low orbit, exploding every military and spy satellite. Similar fireworks burst the phones and computers of all the Kings and their retinue.

It was as if the Kings of the World had disappeared from the face of Dearth. None of their monied supporters could reach them or locate them, nor could the Masters of Dearth contact anyone.

Bank computers were scrambled: all debts were electronically abolished. The Resistance had arisen. The Socialists had surfaced. Dearth could evolve again as Earth. The peoples of the world rejoiced. A first ever truly global holiday was declared in every area of every region of every nation on every continent and island, except of course on Conquerors Island.

Thus began The First Millennium of Peace.

Oh, the peoples hoped! The Kings were mocked as prophetic, for having held their meeting on the Ocean called Pacific.

The mighty Kings were never seen nor heard from again.

With the motors of Conquerors Island having been disabled by the Socialist drone pomelo, the Kings and their consorts drifted aimless upon the Pacific before running aground on a deserted island beside parts of a smashed rusted plane.

Top ruler of the uninhabited island now inhabited, AmeriKing Tyrump ordered that all the boats and all parts of the phony island be dismantled and rebuilt, hammered together into a fortress for protection against Tyrump knew not whom.

"We Kings must show our might!" President Tyrump declared to his fellow Kings in the middle of the vast sea.

"Correct me if I'm wrong," whispered broken AfriKing to maimed EuroKing, "but isn't that what wrecked us here in the first place?"

"Slow down, I'm lost!" shouted IndiaKing. "To whom exactly are we showing our might? To the ocean itself? To the clouds and stars in the sky? To the ground beneath?"

"Spare us your poetry, Gita," said EuroKing to IndiaKing. "Just do what he says. I do, and look how well it has worked for me." EuroKing spread his arms wide, puffed out his chest, and hid his backwards boot behind his other one.

"Your Kremlin walls will never be as big as my wall," said ChinaKing to RussiaKing. "I've got the biggest wall of them all."

"You must be so proud," said RussiaKing to ChinaKing. "But my country is nearly twice the size of your country, even after the breakup. And without all those teeming mouths to feed."

"Stop the claptrap!" shouted AmeriKing Donbo Tyrump. "We need to work as one! You must listen to me and obey! Or do you want some flat-broke fisherfolk in future years to discover our fortress of sunken boats bound together useless, and our scattered remains nothing more than a few bones marked by cannibalism! You ungrateful wretched Kings! I will eat last, I vow!"

"Cannibals?! Where?!" cried IndiaKing.

"Here! Here!" said OceaniaKing, meaning to show obedience and servility to the King of Kings.

ChinaKing yawned.

RussiaKing shrugged.

EuroKing sighed.

AfricaKing groaned and stared out to sea.

Not to worry! Happily for the Kings of the world, their financial betters eventually bailed them out. The real Masters of Dearth, the Corporate Elite, the Chief Executives and their corporate boards tracked the bedrifted Kings to their castaway island and rescued them for their own good.

The corporate governments needed the national governments to protect them. The corporate elite needed their handpicked officials to rule like Kings.

The Kings remained more than happy to oblige, lording over the phony democracies, covering for the big owners, the banker owners, the bowners, the One Percent and its finer fractions in fierce combat against the ever-unruly peoples of Earth.

And so the Kings of Dearth were restored to their ruling perches, increasingly shit-smeared by the Socialists and the Resistance though they were. The battle for Earth continued anew.

V.

No matter how much he might wish, Dineh could not stop dreaming about life and death, death and life on Earth. Maybe his dreams served a real purpose in the end. Maybe the dreams helped create a larger vision of the world and life, of the struggle for survival and resistance, equality and justice, liberty and love, victory and prosperity employed for the greater good.

What did it matter in that dire moment, in the Oval Office, with Death on its way. Was there time?

Dineh had an idea. With the window fast closing before the four nuclear warheads from the US Navy submarine Trident II missile struck that Whitest of Houses and the greater Washington DC metro area, presidential aide Dineh thought he might have an idea for saving what might be saved.

"Mr. President, there is something you can do. You can order the abolition of nuclear weapons. Because as we've learned here today, if we don't abolish nuclear weapons we will all die by nuclear weapons. Today, it's the Texas Fundies who are incinerating a vast city. Tomorrow it could be..." Dineh glanced around. "It could be him!" Dineh pointed at the mangled figure of US House Speaker Thuggy Thug Thuggun. "It could be someone like him who hacks and launches the US arsenal against the world. Or who orders it direct. It could be you, Sir. Or your successor. Live by nukes, die by nukes. There's no need for it, Sir. There's no way to survive it. There is no way the human species can survive the continued existence of nuclear weapons. Mistakes happen. Huge mistakes. You can't leave species-lethal weaponry lying around. We are the dying proof."

"Impossible," said US Secretary of State, Oily Oily Oily. "There is no way to verify any countries' eliminating their nuclear weapons. We could get rid of our nukes, while Russia and China might only pretend to do so and hide theirs instead. Then we would be sitting ducks. And we would never know until it was too late."

"As if it's not too late now," said Dineh.

"That's not true, Oily," said NSA Director Allspy. "We would know. I would know. The

National Security Council would know. Our satellites would know. The directors, staff, and workers of more than a dozen US intelligence agencies would know. Including those in the military."

"It's true," said Joint Chiefs General Krushin Karvin Kilman. "The military would know and does know several times over who has what nuclear capability, including where and why and how. However, why should the US military give up the advantage it has with its superior - and far more numerous - nuclear weapons? We are the greatest, we should have nuclear weapons! Why give up the nuclear advantage just because the Russians' nuclear systems are old and subject to malfunctions and projections of incoming US attacks that don't exist? If they launch in retaliation thinking they are under attack, then we launch before their nukes land. And we launch with far more firepower than they can launch with."

"But then we are all dead! Everyone in the world!" Even President Donbo King Tyrump could see the plain facts in the moment.

"Of course," said General Kilman. "That's the price you pay for power! The point is that we win even though we are all dead. For those keeping score at home, we struck with the biggest punch! We win both a technical decision and a real knockout. We win, even though we die doing so. It has to be declared a victory!"

"By whom!" screamed President Tyrump at his top General. "Who will be left to declare victory?! The earthworms in the ground?!"

"It's not even clear that the earthworms will survive," said Dineh.

"Oh, for God's sake, Dineh. Will you stop with the nature-hugging stuff?!" said President Tyrump. "I'm trying to talk sense to this maniac, this General Kilman defending the nuclear system! And then there's this complete corporate stooge I have for Secretary of State, Oily Oily Oily! Plus this NSA Director Allsee Allhear Allspy who knows everything but helps no one! What kind of lunatic terrorist operation did I stumble onto in winning the God Damned Presidency?!"

"I imagine you picked your own Cabinet, Sir," said Dineh.

"The bankers picked my Cabinet! What do I know?! They sent over the list and I selected most of their top choices, why not? Don't the people who run the world know what they are doing?!"

"They seem to like the road to Oblivion, Sir. It's a very rich road, however short, ultimately. It guarantees that life will be short. But you are in charge, Mr. President," said Dineh.

"Do I look like I am in control of anything right now, Dineh?!" said the President.

"A real shit show, isn't it, Sir?" said Dineh. "A global shit show."

"Filch!" said President Donbo King Tyrump. "Filch it. Filch, filch, filch. Filch it all. Filching filch. What the filch. Filch the filch. Just filch. Filch the filching filched filch. Filch!"

"Sir?" said Dineh.

"Prepare that statement! Dineh, you've got, what, two minutes? No more nukes! I want my grandchildren to be around to have grandchildren of their own!"

"Four minutes," said NSA Director Allspy.

"Don't lie to me, Allspy!"

"Four minutes, Sir. And counting."

"Four minutes to grandchildren. Dineh, you've got two minutes to get me a statement to sign, my final Presidential Order, prohibiting both the future use and also the very existence of any nuclear weapons, and declaring that the US is fully committed to deactivating and abolishing all of its nuclear weapons immediately and simultaneously with all the other - lesser, much lesser - nuclear powers of the world. I'll sign it in pen, on computer, and then in a brief few minutes with my very blood, Dineh. Draw it up."

"Yes, Sir." Dineh typed rapidly and downloaded several pre-existing peace accords and wholesale disarmament treaties as attachments. Dineh held back nothing. They would all die here today in a moment, but maybe the world would live because of their last and final gesture.

Dineh didn't have much time, so he had to move fast, and he attached whatever he thought might be most pertinent to the President's statement, whatever he could access quickly, including this summary oration from MIT professor Knowem Clearsky, titled, "The Alien View of Earth":

If you're an alien with a long stretch of understanding maybe hundreds of thousands of years, and you're watching what's going on on Earth, you would be pretty surprised. About 200,000 years ago, a new species appeared on Earth, Humans, radically different from all others, as we can tell by just looking around. For a long time they kind of just wandered around the earth, called Hunter-Gatherers, hunting, picking fruit, things like that. But about 10,000 years ago, they underwent a big change, started settled agriculture, they started building cities, started expanding, started having wars, developed complex cultures, and during the last 10,000 years they have expanded all over the Earth, from where they already had much more densely settled. In this country for example they emigrated originally from England, pretty much wiped out the indigenous population and conquered a large part of the land. So things continued during the 20th century. They had massive wars of mutual destruction. In 1945, they entered a dramatic new era, the Nuclear Age, in which they had devised means to destroy themselves, and at the same time, though we didn't know it at the time, we now know that at about the same time, a new geological epoch began. It's the period when very dramatic changes took place in the environment, caused by human activity. That's why it's called the Anthropocene, the human geological epoch, in which humans began to radically transform the environment. And now to the point where they are on the verge of destroying themselves.

So going back to this interested alien: what he sees is that this remarkable species that developed higher intelligence is now using it in order to destroy itself and is on the verge of destruction. And that's another fact that the alien might be intrigued by. Humans have tried to unite at various times. In 1945, at the beginning of the Nuclear Age, it was recognized by people who were thinking that we simply have to unite in order to overcome the threat we have created to our own existence. And there was an effort, it's called the United Nations, which at the beginning it was hoped would have promise of moving in this direction, but it was pretty quickly undermined by competing nationalisms. As then, so it is now. US corporations today control about half the world economy, and the US military is more powerful than the militaries of the entire world put together. So US initiatives and actions have been critical. In the early years of the UN, the US used its power to dominate the United Nations and basically to turn it into a battering ram against its enemy the Soviet Union. That changed over the years but not in a way that made the UN a functioning independent force that might bring people together. So during the 1950s other industrial societies began to reconstruct from the war. Decolonization began, so huge parts of the world that had been colonies of the European powers gained some measure of independence. All of that led to a more diversified international system. And US power within the UN, though still overwhelming, began to decline, which the US has resisted or ignored, often with great violence, including invasions, and economic and military massacres. Polls of international opinion show that the greatest threat to world peace is considered to be the United States, with good reason.

So to return finally to the interested alien, it might conclude that the world is doomed if the US continues to lead it to its doom. If the US decides to reverse course, then things could change. But look what happened on the recent US election day, a date that might turn out to be one of the most important in human history, depending on how we react. No exaggeration. The most important news of the day was barely noted, a fact of some significance in itself. The World Meteorological Organization reported that the past five years were the hottest on record. The WMO reported rising sea levels, soon to increase as a result of the unexpectedly rapid melting of polar ice, most ominously the huge Antarctic glaciers. In other words, climate change is spiraling out of control. Another event took place on that day, which also may turn out to be of unusual historical significance for reasons that, once again, were barely noted. On that day, the most powerful country in world history, which will set its stamp on what comes next, had an election. The outcome placed total control of the government – the executive, Congress, the Supreme Court – in the hands of the Republican Party, the most dangerous organization in world history.

The last phrase may seem outlandish, even outrageous. But is it? The facts suggest otherwise. The Party is dedicated to racing as rapidly as possible to destruction of organized human life. There is no historical precedent for such a stand. Is this an exaggeration? Consider what we have just been witnessing. The Republican who won the Presidency calls for rapid increases in use of fossil fuels, including coal; dismantling of regulations; rejection of help to developing countries that are seeking to move to sustainable energy; and in general racing to the cliff as fast as possible. He has already taken steps to dismantle the Environmental Protection Agency. Effects may soon become even more vividly apparent than they already are. In Bangladesh alone, tens of millions are expected to have to flee from low-lying plains in coming years because of sea level rise and more severe weather, creating a migrant crisis that will make today's pale into insignificance. With considerable justice, Bangladesh's leading climate scientist says that 'These migrants should have the right to move to the countries from which all these greenhouse gases are coming. Millions should be able to go to the United States.' And to the other rich countries that have grown wealthy while bringing about a new geological era, the Anthropocene, marked by radical human transformation of the environment. These catastrophic consequences can only increase, not just in Bangladesh but in all of South Asia as temperatures, already intolerable for the poor, inexorably rise and the Himalayan glaciers melt, threatening the entire water supply. Already in India some 300 million people are reported to lack drinking water. And the effects will reach far beyond. One of the difficulties in raising public concern over the very severe threats of global warming is that 40 percent of the US population do not see why it is a problem, since Christ is returning in a few decades. About the same percentage believe that the world was created a few thousand years ago. If science conflicts with the Bible, so much the worse for science. It would be hard to find an analogue in other societies.

It is hard to find words to capture the fact

that humans are facing the most important question in their history – whether organized human life will survive in anything like the form we know – and are answering it by accelerating the race to disaster. Similar observations hold for the other huge issue concerning human survival, the threat of nuclear destruction that has been looming over our heads for 70 years, and is now increasing. It is no less difficult to find words to capture the utterly astonishing fact that in all of the massive coverage of the electoral extravaganza, none of this receives more than passing mention. In popular discussion, the phrase "national security" has come to mean security against military threats almost exclusively, downgrading nonmilitary threats, such as climate change, antibiotic resistant bacteria, or viral epidemics. With military threats, you can see them, you can imagine it. People don't think about it enough. But if you think about it for a minute, you can see that a nuclear attack could be the end of everything. These other threats are kind of slow, maybe we won't see them next year. Maybe the science is uncertain, maybe we don't have to worry about it. Climate change is the worst, but there's others. Take pandemics. There could easily be a severe pandemic. A lot of that comes from something we don't pay much attention to: Eating meat. The meat production industry, the industrial production of meat, uses an immense amount of antibiotics, maybe half the antibiotics. Well antibiotics have an effect: They lead to mutations that make them ineffective. We're now running out of antibiotics that deal with the threat of rapidly mutating bacteria. A lot of that just comes from the meat production industry. Well, do we worry about it? Well, we ought to be. You go into a hospital now, it's dangerous. We can get diseases that can't be dealt with, that are moving around the hospital. A lot of that traces back to industrial meat production. These are really serious threats, all over the place. Take something you really don't think about: Plastics in the ocean, which have an enormous ecological effect. When geologists announced the beginning of a new geological epoch, the Anthropocene, humans destroying the environment, one of the main things they pointed to is the use of plastics in the earth. We don't think about it, but it has a tremendous effect. But these are things you don't see right in front of your eyes. You need to think about them a little, to see what the consequences are. It's easy to put them aside, and the media don't talk about them. Other things are more important. How am I going to put food on the table tomorrow? You've got other things to worry about. It's very serious, but it's hard to bring out the enormity of these issues, when they do not have the dramatic character of something you can show in the movies, with a nuclear weapon falling and everything disappears.

People have been deluded to believe that the Republican winner will do something to remedy their plight, though the merest look at his fiscal and other proposals demonstrates the opposite – posing a task for activists who hope to fend off the worst and to advance desperately needed changes. Exit polls reveal that the passionate support for the Republican was inspired primarily by the belief that he represented change, while the Democrat was perceived as the candidate who would perpetuate their distress. The likely 'change' of the winner will be harmful or worse, but it is understandable that the consequences are not clear to isolated people in an atomized society lacking the kinds of associations, like unions, that can educate and organize.

There are other factors in the Republican winner's success. Comparative studies show that doctrines of White Supremacy have had an even more powerful grip on American culture than in South Africa. And the Democratic party abandoned any real concern for working people by the 1970s, so many people are therefore drawn to their bitter class enemies, the Republicans, who at least pretend to speak their language – a carefully cultivated folksy style, or using little jokes, or acting like regular guys you could meet in a bar. One of the great achievements of the doctrinal system has been to divert anger from the corporate sector to the government that implements the programs it designs, such as the highly protectionist corporate/investor rights agreements that are uniformly mis-described as 'free trade agreements' in the media and commentary. With all its flaws, the government is to some extent under popular influence and control, unlike the corporate sector. It is highly advantageous for the business world to foster hatred for pointy-headed government bureaucrats and to drive out of people's minds the subversive idea that the government might become an instrument of popular will, a government of, by, and for the people. Popular mobilization and activism, properly organized and conducted, can make a large difference. The stakes could not be greater. Earth and its peoples may make a great comeback, depending on how we change. Otherwise, sooner or later, if we continue on the current path, everywhere and all will be rendered uninhabitable, and our history will have come to an end.

Quickly, Dineh put together the Presidential Directive, with attachments ready and prepared. "Almost, hang on!" said Dineh. Standing behind the President's desk and working rapidly on his handheld, Dineh was all but set to send the

Declaration of Nuclear Disarmament and Peace to the President, who was seated at his desk ready to sign the Declaration on his electronic desktop.

"We won't allow it!" screamed a cadre of the President's executing officers who made a frontal and flanking assault on the desk of the President.

CIA Director Creepy Coupy Cutthroat, NSA Director Allsee Allhear Allspy, and the military's Joint Chiefs General Krushin Karvin Kilman had gone off to the perimeter of the Oval Office and enlisted about half the security agents in the room to attack the President, who was spontaneously defended by the security agents standing immediately around him and by assorted others in the room. There seemed to be very little thought at work in the melee. Everyone more or less instinctively reacted. An outsider looking in would have found it very difficult to know who was fighting whom, which side was which. It was crazy and desperate and pathetic and degenerate and terrifying and vicious all at once.

One of the security agents jumped up on the President's desk and emptied his machine gun into the ceiling of the Oval Office, bringing down a hailstorm of plaster, cement, and bullets. When he ran out of bullets, he shouted, "Stop this madness or we are all dead!"

He was immediately killed, cut in half by the fire of another agent, who was then knocked out by a punch to the jaw in the mad crush. It was difficult to get off a targeted shot in the crowded room. Guns were swung as clubs. Fists did their bloody work. Furniture and furnishings were used like sticks and stones, as if a psychotic battle of cavemen from prehistoric times, insane hunters in mad fury in a fancy tomb of a cave.

And then suddenly everyone was thrown to the floor. A shock and boom seemed to lift up the Oval Office and move it to one side.

"The big one?" someone asked.

"No," said NSA Director Allsee Allhear Allspy, staggering to his feet and facing the President still seated in his chair, though thrown back to the windows overlooking the beautiful White House lawn. "We won't feel the big one. It will instantly vaporize us here at ground zero. That blast was Marines trying to smash into this room to get the president out. They won't be able to break though without killing us all, or almost all. In any case, they will soon be vaporized too."

"It is the people farther out who will suffer the most horrible deaths and agony," said Dineh, flat on the floor but now finishing his work on the Declaration of Disarmament and Peace.

"That's the price we must be willing to pay for superiority," said General Krushin Karvin Kilman. "That's the price to win."

"I'm not willing to pay that price," said Dineh. "Anyway, it will destroy everything if we don't stop it. Global annihilation."

"That's the price we must pay for security," said Director Creepy Coupy Cutthroat.

"For secrecy, you mean," said Dineh. "And

for rule by gun and bomb for the benefit of the One Percent. That doesn't make for security. Quite the opposite. Who is secure? Your goddamned violence breeds terror, Coupy. Your terror breeds terror. Nuclear weapons are terror weapons."

"That's the price we must pay to maintain our standard of living," said NSA Director Allsee Allhear Allspy.

"That's not true," said Dineh. "Except for the One Percent, for now. The corporate elite standard of living is being defended, only theirs. Everyone else is being crushed and put at risk, and the world itself is being condemned to total destruction. Condemned to death! What part of 'condemned' and 'to death' do you not understand?"

"We cannot get rid of nuclear weapons!" screamed NSA Director Allsee Allhear Allspy. "I won't allow it! Because then we, the Incorporated Estates of America, can no longer control the world!"

"You don't own the world," said Dineh. "Even if you fine gentlemen think you do."

One of the agents who had been wounded and knocked unconscious during the fighting began to come awake, moaning and crying out in tortured pain. He had been ripped apart and half-gutted by shrapnel. He cried for his mother. Literally. He cried for his mom. Dying, in torturous fear, agony, and oblivion, he called out to her. He cried for his mommy, this condemned creature that was once, mere moments earlier, a powerful soldier now become an unspeakable waif of a ghoul of despair. It was almost too much for some off those in the room to bear. In fact, it was too much. There was suddenly an unspoken undercurrent of people begging for the bomb to hit at once to end it all for those in the room, the beyond be damned.

Dineh tapped his handheld and delivered the documents to the President, who stood up and walked to the electronic face of the presidential desk, where he could sign the Declaration of Nuclear Disarmament and Peace, and transmit the Declaration to the world. Global reactions would pour in instantly. There might be a chance for the world.

The President tried to wipe blood off the computer screen. But before he could sign, the Trident II nuclear warheads from the US submarine hit.

Washington DC exploded.

Carnage, everywhere.

Karnage where Karnage was King.

Washington DC, the Kapital of Krazy Killings, done in, by the Texans.

The self-imposed holocaust poured over the greater Washington DC metro area. The deadly radioactive fallout swept in and out of the city far beyond, killing and fatally poisoning the people and creatures in its mutant path.

CHAPTER FOUR

Death by Dollar

*P*residential Aide Dineh was having a bad day.

Dineh woke on the floor of the Oval Office where President Hilty Crimeton was kicking him in the left side of his ribs with the metallic point of her shoe.

Dineh opened his eyes.

Another blow landed.

Dineh closed his eyes.

"I saw that!" cried President Hilty Crimeton. "You're awake!"

Dineh opened his eyes again. "You're alive," he said.

"Of course I'm alive! You're the one who passed out, not me! Oh, I've been known to hit the floor a few times myself, sure. Now get up! There's money to be made, money, money, money, and more money! Let's make it, Dineh! We have the big meeting to get ready for!"

"Is Washington DC still here?" asked Dineh. "I see you are."

"Dineh, you lunatic! Get up! The state of the

free world is at stake! You know what I mean! I mean the state of my pocketbook!"

"It's all one and the same to you, isn't it?" said Dineh.

"Of course it is, you fool! Now get up, Dineh!"

"I'm ready, Ms. President."

"No, you're not, Dineh, get up! The goddamned Cabinet meeting! How I hate my Cabinet! They are all after one thing: money! You can't hire anybody for anything else anymore!"

"A cabinet meeting?" said Dineh. "Another one?"

"It's practically our first! What do you mean? Honestly, Dineh, when you pass out, you absolutely lose your mind. And your will to work too! You're not very useful then."

"The Devil too works hard for gold," said Dineh. "It's a damn shame." He couldn't get off the floor.

President Crimeton launched a hard kick into Dineh's left shoulder. Then she sat down on the couch. "Dineh, I think I need my medicine."

"I think so too," said Dineh. "Let me get it for you." Dineh crawled toward his workstation where he kept the President's medicine. "I'm alive," he said to himself. "And Hilty Crimeton is President, and she is alive." Dineh had a headache.

"What do you mean, you're alive?" said President Crimeton. "Of course, you're alive. Why wouldn't you be? I'm not working you that hard, Dineh. Don't pretend I am. I've never gone easier on a presidential aide in all my life! You should be grateful. This is my new empathetic, generous, enlightened self."

"May the gods help us," whispered Dineh. He pushed halfway out through the doorway of the Oval Office. "Donbo King Tyrump was never President," he muttered. He crawled into the hallway. "And the Nuclear Disarmament and Peace accord was never signed."

Dineh crawled onward, and pulled himself to his workstation, then reached up into a drawer of his desk and took out a small bottle of nasal spray containing the secret sauce. He thought about using a squirt of it himself, then thought better. There would be no end to it.

"Dineh!"

"I've almost got it."

"Dineh, bring some money with you. Big money. I feel a need coming on. Besides, I want to put a little something in my new coin purse. Isn't it the most beautiful coin purse you've ever seen, Dineh? Don't you think so, Dineh? Dineh?"

Dineh hung on to the nasal spray, and crawled toward the Money Closet. He almost made the door before he had visions of a massacre, of bodies lying in ditches, women and children. He saw the peoples' hopes and dreams destroyed. He saw cultures fragmented, withered, rotted, smashed.

And then a figure stepped over him, from the direction of his workstation to the Money Closet. The figure opened the door and went inside and slammed the door behind him. Dineh recognized the executing officer as the Director of the

National Security Agency, Allsee Allhear Allspy.

"President Crimeton?"

"Do you have my money yet, Dineh?" called the President from her office. Then President Hilty Crimeton came to the doorway of the Oval Office and looked across the hall at Dineh prone before the Money Closet. "Get off the floor, Dineh!"

Dineh tried to explain. And in the moment that President Hilty Crimeton understood that the National Security Agency Director had broken into her Money Closet, and was currently inside, and was doing God knows what, marking bills, no doubt, stealing from her, taking photographs, pocketing as much money as possible, in that moment was when Hilty Crimeton lost it, possibly even more than she ever had before. Her very own money was being stolen, right out from under her nose!

President Crimeton launched a scream so fierce that Dineh lost his hearing. And then he came close to losing his life, as Hilty Crimeton jumped up into the air as high as she could, which was not very high, but high enough, and she came down hard, with the pointed heels of both shoes making contact, flush and full, piercing through the ribcage of her aide, Dineh.

CHAPTER FIVE

Death by Storm

"If I ever dream again, just...kill me," said Dineh to no one in particular.

"Dineh, what are you talking about? Come over here for a moment," said President Donbo King Tyrump. "I need to sign something. But I want you to tell me how it sounds first, see if I've got it just right. I want to send a thank you note to Hilty Crimeton, congratulating her on running a hard-fought campaign. I want to thank her for all she has done for the country setting things up so well and handing it over to me by way of her pitiful run for office. I wonder how I should sign it? What about: 'Your President, Donbo King Tyrump'. How does that sound?"

Dineh shrugged. "You could sign it, 'King Don'."

"King Don! I like it! You blister me, Dineh, you really do. King Kong! King Don! King Bong! No, that's not right," said President Tyrump.

"Thank you, Sir. I do what I can. You lead, I follow. That's all I do."

"Straight to the gates of Hell, Dineh! I know you will follow me anywhere. That's why I keep you around. That's why I keep anyone around. Straight to the gates of Hell! I hear they have tremendous parties in Hell," said President Donbo King Tyrump. "Tremendous."

"I don't doubt it, Sir. And by the 'gates of Hell', Sir, do you by any chance mean, the Pentagon? I pass by there each day on the way to work."

President Donbo King Tyrump smirked. "It's good to be President, Dineh! It's good to be King! King Don! Who would have thought!"

"The world is astonished, Sir."

"I astonish myself, Dineh. I do every day when I look in the mirror. Then when I look at my image on all the magazine covers, and on all the TV shows and computer channels all across the internet, I am astonished again. What success! I love to watch the shows, Dineh. I'm not a Loser at all. I'm a winner! Some people thought I was a Loser, but I wasn't, I won. I showed my Dad. Rest his all-white soul. I showed everyone. No one dares put me down now, Dineh. No one dares laugh anymore, and yet people think they can unmask me. They think they can pull back some invisible curtain and show people who I really am. What curtain, Dineh?! Am I not the first President, the first King of the USA to flaunt the fact that I wear no clothes at all?! Clothes are for Losers, Dineh! You know how corporate culture is, they don't want you to wear any clothes at all on TV. Unless you are a General, Dineh, then clothes are all you can see, the fine fabrics and medals on top of the uniforms, layers of martial bling. TV puts the whole circus of life out there for everyone to see, naked. It would if it could. It tries. Except for the Generals and Cops, Dineh. It seems like every other show is a cop show, Dineh, because the only thing more fascinating to TV than naked bodies is guns. Guns and gore are even more fascinating than God. Bare skin and big guns, that's what got me elected, Dineh! My shiny white skin and metallic gray guns. Oh, and money. Big money. We're a nation of gun-toting rich white nudists at heart! Half the people voted for my finger-in-your-eye circus, and half voted for, okay, more than half voted for my opponent who dresses like a General. Thank God for our beautiful antique Electoral College, Dineh. Half voted for fully-clothed Hilty Crimeton and war with Russia. And half vote for naked old me promising peace in our time, and jobs, and White Lives Matter! You know what I mean. I ran on change! People voted for change! Who cares what kind?!"

"Some lives matter more than others, Sir?"

"Oh, clearly. White ones. Not that you should say so aloud. You just think it. Sometimes we forget which lives matter most. I think we've got it straight now, though, with my election. We don't want things evening up. Who knows what will happen? I suppose anything is fine, as long as I profit. Why again did Hilty Crimeton get a single vote? Maybe they liked her pant suits. Hilty thought she could hide in her secret server, behind her private curtain, where she sold access and influence worth hundreds of millions of dollars for the Crimeton Foundation. Going on billions! Hell, she got away with it - she won the popular vote, if you can believe the count, which I doubt that you can. No one should. I don't. That's my public position and I'm sticking to it. There's more voter fraud than bank fraud, Dineh, who can doubt it, and just between you and me, we know bank fraud is so far off the charts that you can't even track it."

"Candidate Peoples was all over that, Sir."

"Alle Peoples had a point, but you shouldn't say so publicly. It's gutless. And we've got bigger things to worry about. Can you imagine how many frauds showed up to vote this election? Most of Hilty Crimeton's support was fraudulent, that's for sure. Bunch of frauds with votes. Well I won the wonderfully devised Electoral College vote, that's clear. It used to be who you know, now it's how well are you devised, Dineh. Divised, deviced, devised! What's the difference?! Instasnapfacetwit won me the election! There I was naked all over cyberland screaming my ballcap off! The voters, poor schmucks, are trapped in an endless hall of mirrors, no, Dineh? Just looking to get out alive. Crazy nudist politics. Who would've thought? Who should think? Throw in the internet and it's warp speed now. Star Trek, Dineh. I'm pretty good at it. The media made big bucks off my hide, as you were witness. Who knew I could flay myself to victory? I'll probably try to pass legislation with that damned Alle Peoples. Then again, I may not. No idea why he's so popular. He's not even super rich like me and Hilty Crimeton. And his clothes are for crap. Anyway, me and Alle, we are the two most powerful politicians around anymore. Could be we need each other. Alle Peoples will be my biggest political problem going forward, how to deal with him and his supporters, how to neutralize him running for President again in a few years. Alle Peoples is a far bigger problem for me than the Chinese, Dineh. Far bigger. The Socialist Republic of Vermont is out to get me. Alle Peoples is up there in his green hills plotting to take me down. We need to pound Alle Peoples, Dineh. Don't doubt me."

"Everyone is staggered by your victory, Sir. The enormity of it, no one doubts."

"Tremendous. Now, let's do something really happening, Dineh. Forget a border wall, I want to build a border mall! A big beautiful mall, stretching all the way from the Gulf of Mexico to the Pacific Ocean! Bigger and bolder than the Great Wall of China! Visible from space! Visible beyond the galaxy! We'll light it up with colorful strobes! That should hold off the invading Mexican hordes, I would think, and give the Muslims pause. The longest and most profitable mall in the world, one continuous building, 2,000 miles long! We'll surround it with parks and golf courses on either side to make it attractive to money. The walls of the mall will be not merely a single wall, but a double wall of the border! We'll save money. We'll build the double wall mall in a straight line east to west, west to east, it doesn't matter. We'll build it dozens and hundreds of miles above the existing border! Then guess what, Dineh? After my presidential terms are up, I'll personally buy all the land between the new mall border and the old existing border, and then - don't tell anyone - I will secede from the US! Nobody wants that land anyway."

"Sir, there are a number of native peoples there, tribes, and other landowners, who-"

"Indians? Christ, Dineh, what century are you living in? Oh, don't worry, I'll cut a deal, everyone will be happy. I'll be founder of my own new country when I'm done with everything, Dineh. Put that in your pipe and smoke it."

"In my peace pipe, Sir?"

"In whatever pipe, you wish, Dineh. I don't care. My new country will be one big resort, the world's biggest. Everyone will want to move there. True, my country will lie to the south of the border mall wall. So be it. I'm not afraid of the Mexicans, unlike my biggest fans in whitebread America. Gods, Guns, and Gonads, Dineh, it sells! The Mexicans have always worked cheap for me. And when they live in my new country, the Republic of Tyrump, Tyrumpland, or *Tyrump!*®, whatever we name it, they will be so thankful that they will work even cheaper! Cheap labor is what makes this country great, Dineh! And my new country too! Wages are too high! You know it's true. I said it during the campaign. I'll keep my promises, Dineh, as I see fit. Of course I won't live in my new country. I'll merely farm it. I'll live in my tower in New York. The

Mexicans will build me a new tower, twice as tall, and pay for it too with their own blood, sweat, and tears. That's what good work is, Dineh. I'll vacation there. I would move in but I don't think my darling wife Myownia would like it. I think she married Manhattan as much as she married me, back in the day. She's a New York girl now, but we can get it to work, we always do. The first thing we need is to get that border wall mall built to spread the greatness of my name and fame. Okay, so, I don't build anything any more, Dineh. I rent out the use of my name and fame instead. Contractors get a lot of miles out of the great 'Tyrump' brand, Dineh, and they build on their own dime. You can turn a faster buck that way."

"That's very inspiring, Sir. You know how to make everything work."

"And everyone too, Dineh. I don't go to malls, but I know that people like them. And we aim to please, do we not?"

"We certainly aim, Sir. We do take aim."

"Outstanding! It's settled, then, the wall and the future of my country, the Republic of Tyrump. Now, what else?"

"Sir, where to begin? Climate change, the nuclear weapons programs, unemployment, wages, medicare, social security, prisons, drugs, ignorance and illiteracy, war and peace, famine and drought, energy, toxins, infrastructure, all these and..."

"Oh, my God, Dineh, you are boring me to death! The President of this country cannot be troubled by such things. Let the people take care of it. We're a nation of volunteers, Dineh. The people are happy to deal with this sort of thing - what do you call it? - on their own."

"Quality of life? Well, Sir, some leadership might be of use. And some funding. A lot of funding. You see, Sir, if everyone is volunteering, who will be making money to spend, Sir. Who will be able to eat?'

"I'm sure they'll get by, Dineh. If they can't afford cake, let them eat bread. There's a lot of good bread these days. I had a fresh loaf this morning. Wonderful bakeries. The best. Let's promote bread, Dineh. Start a campaign. My darling wife, Myownia, she likes bread too. Make her the pretty face of the campaign, something like, 'Bread for all! It's tasty! And affordable too! Yummm! Good!' How about that slogan?"

"I think we'll leave the advertising to the professionals, Sir."

"Oh screw it, Dineh. You handle the details."

"Really, Sir?"

"Why not? You don't think I'm going to do all the work around here, do you?! I won! Why work?! I'm going to watch the shows and see what people have to say about me! I'm going to tweet until my fingers break! My fingers won't break, Dineh. I have big hands, big strong hands. I can tweet like nobody's business. That's still my job, Dineh. I am the reigning Instafacetwit champion of the world. The underlings will run the country for me. You, for example. You are my loyal retainer, my chief nasal spray operator. You keep the little bottles primed and ready to go, all for me. You are my own private nostril arsenal assistant. You are my go-to guy in the crunch, Dineh."

"I do feel crunched sometimes, Sir. How much of a budget might be had, Mr. President?"

"Budget? For what?"

"For the bread campaign, Sir. For your wife Myownia."

"Oh, for Myownia. Right, right. Oh, well, for Myownia, the sky is the limit. She's sensible. For example, she spent a mere $10,000 on lingerie at Victoria's Secret the last time we visited. And they really try to soak you there. You would be amazed at what you can buy in the back rooms. Frightening stuff. But Myownia is very modest, a very sensible girl. Speak with her. Make sure you get her approval on anything. If I don't like it, I'll have a word with her. She's a very sensible, girl, Dineh. We don't have to worry about her."

"I appreciate your trust, Mr. President. Myownia's campaign for bread for the people will amaze you, I promise."

"No trust, no promises, Dineh. Just do your job as I see fit. *Crystal*?"

"Clear," said Dineh.

"Okay, Dineh. It's time for my bottle. Help an old guy out, will you?"

Dineh coded into the President's desk and selected a small plastic bottle of the President's finest spray. He handed it to the President, who self-administered each nostril.

"Oh! Baby! Now we're talking! Dineh, you're my man!"

Dineh took the bottle from the President who leaned back in his chair and gazed happily up at the white ceiling of the Oval Office.

President Tyrump stared at the big plaster medallion centered on the ceiling depicting the Seal of the President of the United States of America. He was thinking of replacing the Presidential Seal with a giant mirror.

Based on the Great Seal of the United States, the Presidential Seal was the official coat of arms of the US Presidency, at which President Donbo King Tyrump often gazed up and tried to guess its meaning. It showed a bald eagle clutching arrows and olives in its talons and a ribbon in its beak upon which was written in Latin, E. Pluribus Unum, 'One From Many'."

"That's the stupidest thing I've ever seen," said the President to Dineh. "That phrase, 'One From Many', it should read, 'Many From One'. From me and the Presidency flows all."

"It may be too late to have it changed, Sir. If that's what you're thinking."

"Nonsense, Dineh. It's never too late. But don't worry, I wasn't thinking. There will be time enough for thinking another day."

"Certainly, Sir." Dineh walked out of the office and into the adjoining kitchen and placed the little plastic bottle in the recycling bin.

Suddenly, the pomelo appeared and hovered beside Dineh.

"We've got a budget," Dineh said to the pomelo.

"We'll need one," replied Justice Assured of

Wikilooks. "How much?"

"Could be anything. Whatever Myownia doesn't know she's signing off on."

"Myownia, Myownia, Myownia. Wherefore art thou, Myownia?" said the pomelo. "Could work. An unwitting agent of the future. Who could guess? I'll look into it," said Justice Assured.

"Hack away," said Dineh.

"We may have a surprise coming soon," said Justice Assured.

"What is it?" asked Dineh.

The pomelo glittered then suddenly transformed into the image of Justice Assured sitting at his desk touching the screen of his handheld with his index finger.

"We hope to see," said Justice Assured.

His image crackled, then disappeared into the pomelo, which shone brighter than ever.

"What does that mean?" said Dineh.

"We'll see what it means," said Justice Assured.

"Dineh?!" the President called out.

The pomelo disappeared.

"Yes, sir?!"

"Who are you talking to?"

"No one, Sir. Myself, Sir. I'm looking for the Coke."

"You mean the soda pop? It's in the fridge!"

"I'm sure it is, Sir. I'm getting there. Do you want one?"

"No, I'm good, Dineh. Very good. I'm as good as I've ever been. Good as I'll ever be."

"I understand, Sir. I'll be back in a moment. Then we can not think together, Sir. How does that sound?"

"Perfect, Dineh. Perfect. It's all perfect now."

Dineh had to drink a Coke. Or appear to. He took one from the refrigerator and poured more than half of it down the drain of the sink.

Dineh walked back into the Oval Office. "Time for some Coke," he said to President Tyrump.

The President seemed to ignore him. Dineh moved closer to the President's desk and was not surprised to see that the President had fallen asleep in his chair, while staring at the Presidential Seal.

It all depended on which bottle you gave the President. The sleepy time bottle, or the wake you up bottle. Dineh made a mental note again to not get the bottles mixed up, if there truly was a need for the President to be awake.

"You'll be up late again tonight, tweeting," said Dineh to the unconscious recumbent form. "In all your glory." Dineh went back to the kitchen and dumped out the rest of the Coke.

He waited a moment for the pomelo to return, but it did not show.

Then Dineh pulled up a seat at the kitchen table beside the Oval Office. He used his handheld to text a few allies. And there, while the President slept, Dineh continued work on the Popular Plans, for bringing bread and peace to people wherever they may be.

Meanwhile, all the President's officials were

working on very different plans, including plans that they should have known would threaten immediately to bring the whole world crashing down not only on myriad others but also inadvertently on themselves and on all that was left.

Possibly the President's people were not wicked, or not altogether wicked, merely unteachable.

Or, possibly, they were wicked.

And the systems, within which they worked, even more so.

Wicked by design.

To say that Dineh did not know exactly is to say that he knew. He knew. And he worked late into the night.

Unfortunately, Dineh's night was terminated early.

A great foot from the sky came smashing through the ceiling.

It might have been the foot of god, whatever god, any god. By this precarious point in human history there was a long list of great and horrible gods. The great horrible foot in a massive boot kicked Dineh full-on, caught him flush, shot him smashing through the wall, into the Oval Office, and up through the ceiling, smack through the Presidential Seal.

Dineh rocketed into the sky.

He touched the free floating clouds briefly before entering a terrifying descent, a plunge to the grass. Dineh hit near the base of the Washington Monument.

The gods must be fooling, thought Dineh. Kicking him around, sparing his life.

Dark. Alone.

Was it dawn's early light that leaked toward Dineh, or was it a terrible debris?

Was this dawn's breathtaking and glorious approach? Or the incinerating ash and smoke of a pyroclastic flow?

Immobile, Dineh looked past the Washington monument.

He did not know if he could walk.

The thought occurred to him: I need to get to work.

The President demanded no less.

The Resistance demanded no less.

The fate of the world demanded no less.

The day might be near dawn.

But if instead all civilization were on the verge of exploding like a volcano, well, then, what else to do but to go on in the way that he would go on?

Against empire.

For the future.

Dineh stared through the dark at the marble and stone of the Washington monument.

This was no Standing Rock.

This was an alien object stuck like a dagger into the heart of the Earth.

Dineh wondered if every bone in his body were broken.

He wondered if all the blood was going or gone.

He tried to sit up.

He made it.

He looked around.

The Washington monument rose above him like a mutant mountain, like a nuclear stone missile, like a spear pointed at the sky.

Why could this monument not have been a peach orchard instead?

Surely George Washington, experimental farmer, would have vastly preferred living peaches to a giant gravestone of a tomb of a missile of a specter of a weapon of total death?

This was precisely what the thing looked like to Dineh.

That, and it looked stupid. It was a stupid rock thing. It wasn't even a rock.

In fact, the Washington monument looked hideous to Dineh. At least, idiotic.

Dineh admired the incredible craft of its build, mighty, tall and strong, but he despised its imposition upon the land.

Upon the peoples. Upon the lands.

"It's all so stupid," he said. "And monstrous." Dineh stood up. "It's inhuman."

His gaze enveloped the obelisk, the White House, the Capitol, the memorials, the tombs.

Dineh breathed the damp, the cool.

He walked through the mists.

The snow fell softly, gently at first.

And then suddenly it stormed, fast and furious.

What month was this? Late winter? Early spring? Mere weeks after the inauguration? President Tyrump had been in power for a full year by now, a decade, it felt, a century or more, but couldn't possibly be.

Climate change. Dineh recalled that scientists had predicted that as the planet warmed, as both the Arctic and Antarctic collapsed, weather patterns would shift so that late winter and early spring snows would intensify in the eastern US. And may the gods help the rest of the planet.

What climate change Hell might be coming?

Dineh blinked snow out of his eyes. For a moment, he hesitated. He looked ahead as far as he could see into the blinding white.

A person walked through the storm toward him. She was wrapped in snow-covered blankets and made big by the blankets and by the snow piling on. "Dineh," she said, "what are you doing out here?"

"Who are you?" asked Dineh.

"I'm with the camp," she said. "All the people are here."

"There's a camp?" Dineh looked past her.

"Hidden by the storm," she said. "They've all had enough of this shit." She gestured to the White House.

"Yes." Dineh looked with her. "Have you ever seen this much snow?"

"What's behind the snow, that's what matters," said the woman.

"Who's in the camp?" Dineh asked.

"Everyone. Everyone who cares about the future. More every day. And there are camps in every city, county, and town now."

"Do they know what they want?" asked Dineh.

"They want their world back. And they want it back now. And they want more of it. They want all of it for everyone. They want it better than it ever has been before. Way better. Better than could previously even be imagined. Their ideas keep growing, Dineh."

"They want to take over the White House, don't they?" said Dineh.

"That's part of it. The people want power. The people want the power to be people," said the woman. "Long time coming."

Dineh looked to where he worked. "The officials and the executives in and around the White House, the rulers of the world, they're very serious about keeping it for themselves. They think they own it. They think they own the country, the planet. They think they own you, me. They think they are the masters of the world, they think they are the Lords of all. They're very serious about it. They think because they have taken all the money and because they control all the money and because they have taken all the most valuable stuff that they are entitled to make all the decisions. They won't give any of that up. Except tiny bits or whatever cheap little things they might throw out to people to maintain their ultimate power. The One Percent and the One Percent of the One Percent, they will have to be defeated by democracy, by the forces of democracy. So how big is the camp?" asked Dineh. "And how much does it know? And what is it capable of? Achieving democracy for all?"

"Getting closer every day." The woman nodded. "You might want to get back inside now, Dineh. It's all blowing up as we speak. Because of the video. Did you hear? They finally got the video working, at long last."

"The Resistance? The Socialists?"

"Yes. The video, to go with the audio. We can see everything now, no more hidden dealing. We can hear everything of the high officials. There can be no refuge for the rulers anymore, anywhere. No escape for power from the eyes of the people. We've thrown open the doors to the rulers' dens, Dineh, to their power over us."

"No more hidden kicks to the ribs!" said Dineh.

"No more secret deals, secret deployments, secret destruction. It's a step, a needed step forward."

"And then what? Keep going?"

"Dineh, that's why I came looking for you. You went deep into the storm."

Snow fell all around. "This is where we are," said Dineh.

"You left your phone in the Oval Office kitchen. The President has it now, and he's cursing you. He's pissed. He's blaming Justice Assured and Wikilooks. He's blaming the Resistance and the Socialists, and everyone else. You!"

"Everything can be seen?" said Dineh. "Everyone in power?"

"If they so much as wink at each other now,

we can see it. Text? We copy and call out. Email? Download and display. Phone? Broadcast. Word process? Publish everywhere. The peoples' business is going public finally. Imagine that. We are making every act of every banker and every corporate lobbyist visible to everyone. The PR industry is panicking. The executing officers are losing their minds in and around the Oval Office. They can't figure out how they will be able to continue crucifying the people, taking their money, breaking their lives, killing and controlling them with debt, destroying their world. The President wonders where you are, Dineh. He says you abandoned him. He says he needs his bottle."

Dineh and the woman laughed.

"Nice to meet you, Dineh."

Dineh remembered his initial surprise at her familiarity with him. "Do we know each other?"

The woman in the blankets turned and walked into the obscurity of the storm.

"What happens next?!" Dineh called out.

The woman walked back from out of the storm. She stood still in front of Dineh. Snow covered, wrapped in blankets, she reached forward, she gripped his arm.

"You fight," she said. "We're all fighting through this. We have no choice. They're fighting us. That's what happens next. But you knew that. We have to move and grow, Dineh. We have to learn. You learn, you teach, you put your foot down against those who would crush all you hold dear. We learn from each other, we help each other, and if you're a fighter, you fight. Is that who you are?"

"The state has a monopoly on force," said Dineh. "If we fight, there will be a massacre."

"Then there had better be another way," said the woman. "People must move together. Each in their own way. And together."

The storm was swallowing the woman. White layers, waves of white. She gripped Dineh's arm. The storm threatened to bury them both where they stood.

The woman was gone so suddenly that Dineh wondered if she had been real. He couldn't see far through the dark and the storm.

"Dineh!!! Dineh!!!"

Dineh thought he heard screaming from the Oval Office.

"Find Dineh! Bring him here! Get Dineh!"

Dineh reoriented himself.

And then he went forth through snow.

About Author

*T*ony Christini is author of *Homefront* and other works, and co-editor of *Liberation Lit* anthology.

Tony Christini

*"P*ost-election United States. Presidential Aide Dineh is floating between two equally horrifying nightmares: in one he is serving Republican President Donbo King Tyrump, in the other he is being kicked and humiliated by Democratic President Hilty Crimeton. Who really won the last election, who is in charge of the mightiest country on earth? Both leaders appear drugged, both are extremely aggressive, and both are obsessed with power. Dineh is 'dark', he is a Native American, he is plotting a rebellion, trying to save the world. But can he succeed, facing the entire apparatus of political gangsters and thieves?

Tony Christini is at his best. In his novel he is exposing the insanity of empire, its security services and military, its deadly nuclear arsenal. Essential questions are asked and answered, such as: "can the world really survive such a monstrous and racist arrangement?"

Throughout the chapters, things are falling apart. Madness reigns. Compassion, humanism and kindness are all missing from the hearts and minds of the political 'elites'. All this is not hyperbolic: it is real. That is why it is so frightening.

The book has to be read by every man and woman who is still able to question and to resist. The survival of our Planet is at stake. And

Christini's voice is both outraged and determined. It calls for action. It demands action. It is precisely what a political novel is obliged to be during the moments of total darkness.."

~ *Andre Vltchek*
Author of *Aurora, Point of No Return*

"*I* had a blast reading *Empire All In: A Novel of the Trump Era*. Tony Christini takes us on a wild ride—as funny as it is frightening. Troubling dreams become a full-blown nightmare as the US falls, like a drunk at the end of a disastrous party, into the arms of President Donbo King Tyrump. Is Christini writing satire or filling us in on our future? Can fiction compete with the bizarre, surrealistic, dystopian, this-can't-be-true US presidential election? I'd thought not until I read Christini's *Empire All In: A Novel of the Trump Era*."

~ *Mark Brazaitis*
Novelist, Professor at West Virginia University

www.ingramcontent.com/pod-product-compliance
Lightning Source LLC
Chambersburg PA
CBHW022028260626
47156CB00017B/832